Amish Widow's Faith

Expectant Amish Widows Book 3

Samantha Price

D1523214

Chapter 1

*Blessed is the man that walketh not in the
counsel of the ungodly,
nor standeth in the way of sinners, nor sitteth in the
seat of the scornful.*
Psalms 1:1

Emily Kauffman couldn't help feeling pleased
with herself as she watched Harriet Yoder and
Michael Steiger get married. Normally the couple's
families would have taken up the first few rows at
such an event, but Emily sat right in the second
row directly behind Harriet's mother.

Emily's father, along with her good friend, Tom,
had both warned her she'd been interfering when
she was matchmaking them, but the result spoke
for itself. While the deacon said a prayer, she turned
to look at Tom and when she caught his eye she
gave him a big smile. Tom was opposed to her new
practice of matchmaking even more so than her
father was. Before Emily turned back around, she

caught sight of Luke Cramer sitting right next to Tom. He would be the perfect man to find a woman for. And what better woman than her sister?

Now swiveling her head in the opposite direction, she looked over at Deborah who was sitting two rows behind. Her dear sister, Deborah, was five years older than she was and had tragically lost her husband only days after they found out they were to be parents.

Even though Deborah claimed she would never marry again, Emily knew that was the best thing for her especially with the baby coming along. A baby would need two parents.

When old Albert Schroder stood up to sing a hymn, Emily turned to the front and closed her eyes and listened to his deep soothing voice. She had to put a clever plan into place to bring Deborah and Luke together. With her sister's current attitude and stubborn nature, it wasn't going to be easy to have her see Luke's good points. Deborah's late husband, Caleb, had been independent and determined, and then there was Luke who kept to himself and still lived with his parents at nearly thirty. All Luke needed was a little confidence, Emily was certain of that.

After a long sermon by the bishop, three hymns, and two prayers delivered by the deacon, the bishop announced that Harriet and Michael were married. Still puffed up with pride that the wedding was entirely due to her and her alone, Emily sat and waited until everyone moved out of Harriet's parents' house where the wedding had taken place.

Tom kneeled on the bench in front of her and leaned toward her. "I suppose you're feeling pleased with yourself."

"Is that your way of acknowledging that this wouldn't have happen if it weren't for me?"

"What I really think, if you want to know, is that we must be thankful that their wedding happened even though you interfered." He added, "In spite of your carryings on and meddling."

Emily's mouth fell open in shock. "What? They'd never even talked to each other before I arranged for it to happen."

"*Gott* would've found a way to get them together."

"So now you admit they're a good match?" She smiled figuring he'd have to agree, but he just shook his head and sighed. "Why is it so hard for you to admit that I was right and you were wrong?"

He grimaced. "What was I wrong about?"

She stood up. "You didn't see them together; admit it."

He stood to his full height of six feet two inches. "It wasn't like that, though, Emily."

Once she had her hands on her hips, she held her chin high. "Wasn't it? Then what was it like?" Emily could see he was holding back a grin.

"It's not that I didn't see them together, but I just didn't not, not see them together. Do you see what I mean? I don't go around sticking my nose into other people's lives." He pressed a finger onto her nose and she swiped at his hand, but she wasn't quick enough to hit it.

She glowered. "And that's what you think I'm doing?"

"That's what I *know* you're doing."

"*Jah*, but you make it sound like a bad thing. Look how happy Harriet and Michael are now. And last year it was Wendy and Bryce, and now they have a *boppli* on the way."

Tom shook his head and folded his arms across his chest. "Who have you got your sights set on now? I'm guessing from the look in your eyes and going by your latest victory you're planning for another marriage for some poor unsuspecting souls?"

She lifted her chin. "It just might be you."

He chuckled. "It better not be. You start messing about in my life and I'll tell your *vadder* and he'll lock you in your room for a week. You might as well tell me what you've got planned. I know I'll hear all about it sooner or later."

Emily's face lit up and she turned around to see if her sister was still nearby. Seeing that she was nowhere about, Emily leaned in, and spoke quietly, "I was thinking of Deborah."

"Your *schweschder?*"

Emily nodded.

Tom stepped back. "Now you're completely overstepping boundaries. What makes you think she'd even be interested in getting married in her condition?"

"She's been married before so it shows she's not totally opposed to the idea."

"She's only just lost Caleb and she's expecting. I'd say marriage is the last thing on her mind."

Emily raised her eyebrows. "And what does that mean?"

"That means that there's even more reason why you should leave her alone."

"But don't you think that Luke would be perfect for her?"

"Why don't you leave it up to her to decide that? If you want to know what I really think, I don't see that Luke would be suitable. He's not mature enough for her." He shook his head. *"Nee,* I just don't see the two of them together."

"Sometimes people don't know what's best for them; especially people like Deborah."

Tom frowned. "Especially like Deborah? What does that mean?"

"She has a closed mind. When she thinks a certain way it's very hard to make her see differently."

"What you need to do is find yourself something productive to do with your time. Then you wouldn't be messing about in other people's lives. And that's what I think." Tom nodded his head sharply and walked right out the door.

I'll show you. When Emily saw that the men were starting to move the wooden benches out of the house to make way for the food tables, she headed outside to look for Deborah.

With a quick scan of the crowd, she saw Deborah at a refreshment table talking to their father, and Luke was in a conversation with a group of men on the other side of the yard. *There's no time like the present,* Emily told herself before she made her way over to her sister.

"What did you think of the wedding?" Emily asked when she was beside Deborah.

After pouring herself a cup of meadow tea,

Deborah answered, "I think it was much the same as every wedding. Why? Do you think this one was particularly exciting?"

"I'll leave you two girls to it." Their father turned and walked away.

"I just thought they made a particularly good pair." Emily reached for a cup.

"That's only because you brought them together."

"*Jah,* I did." Emily poured herself a cup of the sweet chilled meadow tea, and then pulled on her sister's arm. "Let's head over this way a little. I don't want Mrs. Hostetler to see me because she'll have me doing the washing up afterward. She doesn't like me."

Chapter 2

Blessed is the man that endureth temptation: for when he is tried, he shall receive the crown of life, which the Lord hath promised to them that love him.

James 1:12

Deborah King sat by herself at the wedding of Harriet Yoder and Michael Steiger. Her sister had insisted on sitting in one of the front rows, even though Deborah had told her that is where family members sat. Emily was stubborn like that. More than anybody else at the wedding, Emily was pleased to see them getting married; she was convinced it was all due to her matchmaking.

It was the first wedding Deborah had been to since her husband had gone home to be with God. She tried her best to be happy with the life they'd had, and the blessings of the time they'd spent together, rather than dwelling on the times that they would never have. She looked down at the ever-expanding bump under her dress. Caleb would never see their baby's first steps, or be there for Christmases or birthdays. Who would instruct their child in right from wrong? She was well aware that their baby's future rested solely in her hands.

She looked over at the happy couple who were looking adoringly into each other's eyes. That was a feeling she remembered well; the feeling that nothing else mattered when she was in Caleb's arms. She blinked back tears and knew she had to be strong. Having other people sympathize with her made her feel much worse and that's exactly what would happen if anyone saw her looking gloomy or teary-eyed. A false front is what she needed to put up.

Once the deacon began his prayer, most everyone closed their eyes. Deborah noticed that Emily had glanced around to look at someone to the right of her. Deborah followed her gaze and saw her exchanging glances with Tom. Not long after that, Emily's head swiveled to look in her direction.

Tom was a good friend of their father's, even though there was a distinct age difference. Tom was in his late twenties and their father was in his early sixties. Their friendship had begun over woodworking years before, and now they spent hours talking together while they whittled wood in the family's barn. Tom was always over at the house.

Deborah closed her eyes so Emily wouldn't see that she'd had hers open. Slowly opening her eyes, Deborah looked to see that Emily was now facing straight ahead. She glanced to her side to look at Tom. Was there something going on between Tom and Emily that she knew nothing about? She noticed Tom was now staring at Emily; she was certain that's who he was looking at.

Her mind drifted again to Caleb. *Always look for the good in everything,* is what he always used to say to her, and now she did just that. She had no choice but to carry on so she would be a fit mother for her child. After having Caleb taken away from her so suddenly, she had learned to thank God for the blessings in her life. Apart from her mother dying when she was five she'd had no struggles or tough times, and things had always gone smoothly for her, but she'd rarely stopped to say a silent prayer of gratitude for what He'd done for her. Now, she was conscious of giving thanks daily.

Due to Caleb's illness, Deborah and Caleb had lost their home and had moved in with her father a year ago.

Once Harriet and Michael were pronounced married, the happy couple walked outside, and then everyone stood to follow. Just as Deborah was about to leave, she saw that Tom was leaning over talking to Emily. *Jah, I'm certain there is something going on between those two.*

Deborah joined her father at the refreshment table, wondering how much longer they had to stay at the wedding. She wanted nothing more than to go home and have a nap.

Chapter 3

But the fruit of the Spirit is love, joy, peace,
longsuffering, gentleness, goodness, faith, Meekness,
temperance: against such there is no law.
Galatians 5:22

The next night, Tom was over at Emily and Deborah's house as usual. Because of the cooler weather, Tom and the girls' father whittled their wood in front of the fire rather than in the barn where they usually did such things.

"I hate it when they do that in the house," Emily said to Deborah as they sliced the vegetables at the kitchen table.

"It does give *Dat* an interest."

Emily picked up a carrot stick and nibbled on it. "I suppose so, but I'm the one who has to go around and pick up all the wood shavings off the floor when they've finished."

"They're doing it on an old sheet so they shouldn't make too much mess."

"They just annoy me, that's all. I was thinking only this morning, why don't we have Luke Cramer to the *haus* for dinner one night?"

"Jah that would be a good idea. And his parents?"

Emily screwed up her nose. *"Nee.* I was thinking just Luke."

Placing the pot of peas down onto the table, Deborah frowned at her sister. "Why wouldn't you invite his parents?"

Knowing she had to be careful with her next response, Emily kept her eyes on the carrots in front of her. "Oh, I don't know, I just think it would be nice to have Luke here by himself." Emily could feel Deborah staring at her.

"You're not interested in him, are you?"

Emily laughed. "I'm not certain. What do you think about him?"

"It's not what I think about him, Emily. If you like him, of course, have him here for dinner. He's a man that I think has been overlooked by the young women in the community."

Things were going as planned and Emily tried

not to smile. "And why do you think that is?"

"Probably because he's quiet and a little bit shy."

"And there's nothing wrong with that," Emily insisted.

"You don't have to convince me of anything."

"Nee that's not what I'm trying to do. What I mean is I'm glad you see that he's been overlooked. What did you think of him before you and Caleb got married?"

"I didn't think of him in any particular way at all." Deborah looked across at her sister. "Does it matter what I think of him, if you like him?"

Emily whipped her head up to look into her sister's eyes. "I don't like him, not like that. It's just that I've often wondered why he's still single."

"The last thing I heard was that you're not interested in marriage. You told me you want to stay here and look after *Dat* forever. Do you still think that way?"

"I haven't changed my mind about that. I was just thinking it wouldn't hurt to get to know Luke a little better." Emily studied her sister's face as

Deborah concentrated on shelling the peas. *Does she have any hint that I'm trying to match her and Luke together?*

Deborah suddenly looked up and caught her staring at her. "What?"

"Nothing; you just seemed to be concentrating a little too intensely on shelling the peas."

"I was just thinking who would be a suitable woman for Luke and I can't think of one person. He's just so quiet and I know that many people think he's a little odd."

"He's not odd at all," Emily insisted.

"You like matching people together, who would you choose for him?" Deborah asked.

Emily tapped a carrot stick on the table and gazed up at the ceiling. "It would need to be someone very special because he's so sweet and kind."

"So you're not interested in him yourself, then?"

"Nee." Emily made a clicking sound with her tongue. "I can tell he has a lot of good qualities."

Their father poked his head through the kitchen door. "How far away is dinner?"

"About an hour," Emily answered.

"How about a nice hot cup of tea for your poor old *vadder* and one for Tom?"

"Of course, *Dat.* I'll bring them in to you." Deborah rose to her feet and headed to put the pot on the stove. When Deborah sat back down, she said, "Are you thinking of bringing a single girl over here when Luke comes to dinner?"

"*Nee* I think we should get to know him a little better before I try to find somebody for him."

Deborah nodded. "I think that would be a good idea."

"Deborah, do you think you would ever get married again?"

Deborah exhaled deeply. "I don't think it would be fair. Caleb and I had something special, something that would never be repeated. Every other man would fall short if I compared anyone with him. I do get a little sad sometimes, and a little lonely. I've got no one to share the excitement of my child with."

"You have me. I'm excited about being an aunt."

"I know, but it would be nice if Caleb was still around. Sometimes having this *boppli* makes me feel even more alone."

As Deborah wiped a tear from her eye, Emily knew she was doing the right thing in matching her with Luke. If Deborah married Luke, she would have a father for her baby and wouldn't feel alone.

When both girls heard the water in the pot bubbling on the stove, Emily said, "I'll make the tea for them."

Deborah sniffed. "*Denke*, Emily."

Emily leaned over and kissed Deborah on her forehead. "Don't be sad. You'll see Caleb again one day."

Deborah nodded. "You know, I wish *Mamm* were here. I really need her right now." Tears fell down Deborah's face. Both girls rarely talked about their mother without shedding tears.

Emily put her arm around Deborah. "She's still around. I feel her sometimes. I'm certain she's watching over us." Emily reached into her sleeve, pulled out a clean handkerchief and handed it to

Deborah.

"Denke," Deborah said while she dabbed at the corners of her eyes. "It's hard to be strong sometimes. And I don't know whether to block all reminders of Caleb, or whether to think about him. It's certainly easier to block him out of my mind. When I think about him, I just get so sad and sometimes; I feel like I can't cope."

While Emily leaned over Deborah in an embrace, she had no idea what to say to comfort her. She had no clear memories of their mother as she'd died when Emily was only months old, but she did remember the essence of her.

Deborah sniffed. "I'm all right now. I don't want *Dat* to see I've been crying. It'll only upset him."

"Do you think you should hide your feelings from him?"

"I have to, otherwise if he gets sad it will make me feel even worse."

Emily stood straight and took her arm away from her sister. "Why don't you go and wash your face in the cold water outside? If he sees your eyes are red, just say maybe you've got a cold coming on."

"*Denke,* Emily. I'll do that."

Chapter 4

LORD, thou hast heard the desire of the humble:
thou wilt prepare their heart, thou wilt cause
thine ear to hear:
Psalms 10:17

Once Deborah was out of the kitchen, Emily poured tea leaves into the pot, poured the boiling water over them, and gave it a stir. After she arranged the plain white china tea-set onto a tray, she took it out to her father and Tom. Emily was certain her father would complain about no cookie with his tea, but that would spoil his dinner.

As soon as she set the tray down, she noticed splinters flying in the air as they whittled away on their carvings. Emily placed her hands firmly on her hips. "*Dat,* can't you see the mess you're making?"

Her father swiveled his head to look around the room. "Tom and I will fix it when we finish."

"That's what you always say and you never do

it," she grumbled.

Tom looked up at her. "We will, Emily. We will."

Totally disgusted with how they were treating the room she'd only cleaned the day before, Emily headed back to the kitchen to see if Deborah was back inside. She was back and sitting down at the kitchen table.

"They're making a mess out there again?"

Too angry to speak, Emily nodded.

"I suppose that can't be helped; it's too cold for them to do it in the barn."

Emily shook her head at her sister. "Sometimes I think you're far too nice, Deborah."

"How can someone be too nice? Don't answer that. I know you'll have a big long answer about how people can be a little bit nice, too nice, or not nice enough. Anyway, they're not hurting anything in a permanent way. They're just making a big mess and that can be fixed." Deborah dabbed at her eyes.

"They said they would clean it up themselves, so I'm going to hold them to it."

Later, when dinner was ready, Emily called everyone to the table. Before everyone served themselves from the bowls in the center of the table, they closed their eyes and said their usual silent prayer of thanks for the food.

"Seems like everyone enjoyed themselves at the wedding yesterday," the girls' father said.

"Jah it was a very enjoyable wedding," Tom added.

"And I thought they made a lovely pair," Emily said. *"Dat,* I was thinking of having Luke Cramer over for the evening meal one day this week."

"That's a good idea. And his parents?" her father asked.

"Nee, he's not a *bu,* he's a grown man. He doesn't need his parents to come with him."

Her father frowned. "He still lives with his parents. What would be the harm having them to dinner as well?"

Emily grew annoyed when she saw Tom smiling. She glared at Tom, and when he caught her eye, he raised his eyebrows. He seemed delighted that her father wanted Luke's parents to come to dinner as well. "How would you feel if you lived with your parents and no one invited you anywhere by yourself, *Dat*? He's his own person. He just happens to live with his parents, which I think is a *gut* idea because he's probably got lots of *geld* saved; probably even enough to buy his own home." She smiled broadly and looked at Deborah thinking she'd appreciate a man who had saved enough money to buy his own house.

Tom said, "Are you going to ask him for a loan?"

When Emily scowled at Tom he laughed and her father looked confused.

Her father asked, "What do you need money for, Emily?"

After shooting Tom a look of disapproval, she answered, "*Nee, Dat,* I don't need any money. I'm just saying I'm certain Luke wants to be treated like a man, and as a separate person from his parents. *Nee* wait, everyone's confusing me. What I said just then was all mixed up. How would you feel, *Dat,* if you were nearly thirty and still living with your parents and no one invited you anywhere by yourself?"

"*Nee,* that wouldn't be *gut.* At thirty he'd be too old to go to the singings." Her father waved a fork in the air. "Do as you wish. Invite anyone here, I don't mind."

"*Jah, Dat,* I will." Emily looked over at Tom to see him shake his head at her.

"Excuse me for a moment," Deborah said as she stood up to leave the room.

When she was out of the room, Tom whispered, "I really don't think it's a good idea what you're trying to do."

Emily whispered back, "It's for her own good."

Her father joined in the whispering, and asked, "What is?"

Tom explained, "Your youngest *dochder* has the idea that her oldest *schweschder* should be matched with Luke."

"Ah, is that what you're trying to do, Emily?"

"*Jah* and I don't see anything wrong with that."

"I'm guessing you haven't mentioned anything

of this to Deborah?" Tom asked.

"Nee, I haven't, and I want you both to be quiet about it. And I don't want you to be snickering about Luke in front of her."

"Why would we do that?" Tom asked.

"I'm not saying you would, I'm just saying *don't."*

Emily's father looked at Tom and they gave each other a look, which Emily knew meant they both thought she was quite mad. She knew they didn't approve of her matchmaking ways, but neither had they thought it was a good idea for her to match the last couple together and that had worked out brilliantly. "Sh! She's coming back."

When Deborah sat back down at the table, she looked at everyone in turn. "Why did everyone stop talking when I came back into the room? Were you talking about me?"

Emily gulped. "We were talking about Luke and what a *gut mann* he is."

Deborah look down at her food and picked up her fork. Emily wasn't entirely convinced that

Deborah believed what she'd said, but at least she didn't ask any more about it.

"This is a lovely meal, girls," their father said.

"Totally *wunderbaar*," Tom agreed.

* * *

When dinner was over, Deborah went to bed early, amidst her father and Emily arguing about the woodchips scattered around the living room. Slumping onto her firm mattress, she pulled her prayer *kapp* off, and then unbraided her long hair. After she changed into her nightgown, she slipped between the covers and closed her eyes. Nights were the times when she missed Caleb the most. Her hand wandered to the other side of the bed to feel a cold sheet where once she would have felt the warmth of her husband beside her.

The warm glow of the gaslight comforted her somehow, but she knew she wouldn't be able to sleep if she left it on. Once she'd flicked the light off the stillness of darkness swept over her; she was only too aware that she was in the bed alone. She knew she had to be grateful to have her father and sister close, but how she craved her mother to be around, especially now that she was soon to have a child. Her mother would have guided her along the way and told her what to expect.

It hadn't been easy growing up without her mother, but her father had done the best he could. Their mother had died of pneumonia when Deborah and Emily were young girls. Deborah had vague memories of hanging onto her skirts, and her mother singing to her at night, but Emily had only been two months old and had no memories of their mother at all.

Their father had taught them to be independent from a young age, and for that, Deborah was grateful. One thing Deborah knew was that she had to come up with a plan to stop Emily before she went too far with her plans of matching her with Luke. It simply wouldn't do. Emily was being obvious about it while thinking Deborah wouldn't know what she was up to.

Blinking up at the dark ceiling while trying to fall asleep, she couldn't help but be bothered by her sister's secret plot. The best way to deal with Emily was to ignore what she was trying to do – pretend not to notice. If she'd told Emily she knew what she was doing, it would lead to a large discussion and most likely an argument and at this point in her life she didn't want any more disruptions.

Maybe she should beat her sister at her own game and try to match her with Luke instead, seeing that Emily thought he would make such a good husband. She giggled into her pillow at the thought.

Chapter 5

All scripture is given by inspiration of God, and is profitable for doctrine, for reproof, for correction, for instruction in righteousness:

2 Timothy 3:15

Over breakfast the next morning, Emily wasted no time in talking about Luke again.

"Why don't we visit Luke today around the time of the midday meal. I'm sure he'd come home to eat. What do you say? And while we're there we can invite him for dinner."

"I suppose we could as long as *Dat* doesn't want us to do something around here."

Both girls looked at their father.

He stopped eating and looked up at them. "Since when do either of you need my permission to do anything? You're grown women by now."

"Well let's do it," Deborah said. "Shall we make it Friday for him to come to dinner? That will give us time to cook something really special."

"Okay, Friday it is."

Their father shook his head. "You'll have to find out if that suits him first before you go making plans. You don't want to scare the poor man away."

"How would we scare him away, *Dat?* It's only dinner."

Their father shook his head once more and kept silent. He was used to going along with whatever his daughters wanted. He'd retired ten years ago when he and his two brothers had leased their farm to another Amish family. His share of the income was just enough to keep their household since they grew much of their own fruit and vegetables, and kept chickens.

Deborah had moved back into the family home when, due to mounting medical bills, she'd had to sell the home that she and Caleb had bought together. The community had rallied around and held fund-raisers to pay for Caleb's medical expenses. He'd had an illness that baffled the doctors. They'd put it down to being one of the Amish genetic diseases that they still didn't know much about. It was related heart problems that had ended his life. Deborah could only pray that their child would not be affected by the same illness.

Once they cleaned up after breakfast, they hitched the buggy to head over to Luke's parents' house. Luke was the oldest of five brothers and the only one living at home. One of his brothers had left the Amish, and the other three were married.

"We're going to be far too early," Deborah said as the buggy drew closer to Luke's house. "Didn't we plan to arrive for the midday meal?"

"We can talk to Mrs. Cramer and find out more about Luke. All *mudders* like to talk about their *kinner.*"

"Even so, it's going to be three or four hours before he comes home. I don't like staying there for so long."

"Shall we go somewhere rather than turning back and going home?"

"We could go to the farmers market to get some ideas on what we'll cook when Luke comes for dinner," Deborah said.

"Okay. Do you want to do that, then?"

Deborah nodded.

Fifteen minutes later, Emily drove right into the parking lot at the farmers market. After securing the buggy, they were about to make their way inside when they saw Mrs. Cramer walking towards them.

"Mrs. Cramer, we were just on our way to see you after we finish up here," Emily said.

Mrs. Cramer's face lit up. "That's *wunderbaar*. I just bought a cake we can have. It's an orange cake and it's Luke's favorite. We don't often get visitors now that it's only Luke living at home."

Emily giggled a little too loudly.

"I'll go home now and finish that soup I started this morning," Mrs. Cramer said.

"And Luke will be there too?" Deborah asked.

"He comes home at midday every day; I don't see why today would be any different." Mrs. Cramer chortled.

Emily looked down at the bags in Mrs. Cramer's hands. "Do you want some help to your buggy with those?"

"Nee. I'll see you girls soon." After the girls said goodbye, Mrs. Cramer hurried toward her buggy.

"She seems pleased we're coming to her place."

"She does," Deborah said as they continued on to the markets.

"Why did you ask if Luke was going to be there? Now she knows we're coming to see him and not her."

"She wouldn't know that for certain and anyway isn't that why we're going there? So what does it matter? Also I know that you're trying to match me with Luke, and you can forget it."

Emily sighed. "Why did you agree to come, then? And now after what you've said to Mrs. Cramer about Luke being there she might get the wrong idea and think that one of us likes him."

"Well she wouldn't think it was me." Deborah placed her hands on her belly.

"There's nothing to stop you getting married again, Deborah."

"There isn't, but *Dat* never did and he's been happy enough."

35

"You don't have to make the same choice that he did."

Deborah groaned.

"What have I said now?"

"Let's just not talk about me and Caleb."

"Why not? I'm your *schweschder* so we should be able to talk about everything."

"Some things are okay for us to talk about but not that. Not yet, it's too soon. You'll make me start crying again."

"Okay. Let's go buy something that we can take to Mrs. Cramer's."

"All right. I do hope that Luke will be there," Deborah said.

"Why the sudden interest in him?"

Deborah laughed. "You started it. I'm just interested to know why he's not married yet and why he's still living at home."

"There's nothing wrong with him living at home. I think it's nice how he's there to look after his parents."

"Really? Can't they look after themselves?

They're not that old," Deborah said.

"I'm certain that they still need help running the orchard."

"I think his brothers help as well."

"I didn't know you knew that much about them," Emily said.

"I don't really. Do you think he's handsome, Emily?"

"Jah. I think he's okay. And he's tall, well-mannered, and also he's hard-working." As they walked down the aisles of the cake displays, Emily paused and pulled on Deborah's arm. "Why are we here looking at cakes? Mrs. Cramer said she had apple cake, orange cake, or something or other. We should take something other than cake."

"Okay. Like what?"

"We could take an apple pie that she could use for the evening meal. I don't think she's much of a baker from what she said."

"I think they're down this way," Deborah said, pointing a couple of aisles over.

Emily suddenly tugged on Deborah's arm. "Look

over there; it's Tom! What's he doing here?"

Deborah turned to look where Emily was staring. "It's not unusual to see him here; most of the people we know come here."

"Jah, but not Tom."

"Don't be silly. Everyone has to eat."

Instead of listening, Emily was on her tiptoes peering over to get a better look at what Tom was doing. "I think he's here with Ruth."

"Just because he's standing next to her doesn't mean he's here with her. That's how rumors start."

Emily grabbed Deborah's arm again and pulled her over to the end of the aisle, closer to Ruth and Tom. "Ruth Hershberger," Emily mumbled.

Deborah sighed. "It doesn't mean there's anything going on between them if that's what you're thinking."

"Why isn't he in his store working?"

"It's not far from here. Maybe he's grabbing something to eat."

When Tom turned his head slightly, Emily pulled Deborah down so hard she had no choice but to crouch down with her.

"Careful. Don't jolt me so much. What are you doing? People are looking at us."

Emily whispered, "I don't want him to see us."

"You're being silly."

"I'm not. I just want to see what he's up to." Emily raised herself up slightly. "Okay they're on the move." With a tug on Deborah's sleeve, she stood up.

"You're not going to follow him, are you?" Deborah asked.

"Just until I can figure out what he's doing."

"It's really none of your business, Emily."

Emily either didn't hear or didn't want to hear because she was now five paces in front of Deborah and moving quickly.

When Deborah had caught up, Emily whispered to her, "I think they've definitely come here together."

"You can't say that for certain."

"He told me he wasn't interested in anyone. That makes me cross. He's over at our *haus* nearly every day so how come he hasn't mentioned Ruth once?"

"There are some things people prefer to keep to themselves." As usual, Deborah's words fell on deaf ears.

"Why would he be interested in her? She's far too old for him."

"I don't think she is."

"Tom told me he's not interested in getting married," Emily repeated.

"And when did he tell you that?"

"Some time ago."

"Maybe he's changed his mind now. People are allowed to do that, you know."

"Look at them. It looks like they're picking out vegetables together. Do you think she's going to cook for him or something?"

"You could find out right now. Walk up to them and say hello."

"We could never do that, Deborah. *Nee* he must never know we saw him. He must never know that we know about Ruth."

"Do you think you might be a little jealous?"

Emily's mouth fell open and then she frowned at her sister. "Never! He's like our *bruder.*"

Deborah smiled at her sister's reaction. "Maybe he's not working today. Why don't we walk over to his store and find out?"

"That's a great idea, Deborah. We'll go back and get that apple pie and then go on to Tom's store. They'll know whether he's supposed to be working today. And we'll still have time left over before we have to be at Mrs. Cramer's *haus.*"

Chapter 6

Let the words of my mouth, and the meditation of
my heart, be acceptable in thy sight, O LORD, my
strength, and my redeemer.
Psalms 19:14

Deborah was certain Emily was a tiny bit jealous that Tom was spending time with another woman. Maybe they were just good friends or maybe there was something else between them. Lately Deborah had suspected that there really was more to Emily and Tom's relationship than simply friendship. Tom certainly spent a lot of time at the house with their father. The more Deborah thought about it the more she put the pieces together; maybe the way Tom and Emily teased each other was hiding their true feelings.

"Get a move on, Deborah. You're so slow."

"See how fast you are when you're eight months pregnant."

"That's something I'll never be," Emily said.

"I haven't been here in quite a while," Deborah said once they were right outside Tom's store. "It seems bigger than I remember."

"*Nee.* It's just the same as always." Emily took a step back. "You go in first."

After she grunted at her sister, Deborah pushed the glass door open. The first person they saw was Harold Hershberger who waved at them from the back of the store. They made their way to him. Most of the people Tom employed were Amish people from their community, and all the furniture was sourced from local Amish craftsmen.

After they exchanged greetings with Harold, Deborah asked whether Tom might be in.

"He was here a minute ago, but he stepped out." Harold looked from one sister to the other. "Do you want to leave a message for him?"

"You don't happen to know where he went, do you?" Emily asked.

"He doesn't tell me where he's going. I can help you if you're looking for a piece of furniture."

"*Nee.* We just wanted to talk to him, that's

all," Emily said looking over her shoulder at the entrance to the store.

"*Denke,* Harold." Deborah began walking out of the store hoping that Emily would follow. She did. Once they were clear of the store, Deborah said, "Let's just go to Mrs. Cramer's *haus.*"

* * *

As Emily drove the buggy toward the Cramer property, she kept a watch on the fields to see if she could spot Luke.

"You looking for Luke?" Deborah asked.

"*Jah,* and I can't see him anywhere about. I didn't think he would be too far away from his *haus.*"

"Maybe he's way over on the other side behind the *haus* where the orchard is. She did say he comes home for the midday meal, so don't worry; he'll be there."

When the girls had secured the buggy, they

walked up to the house and knocked on the door. It was a large white house and surrounding the deck was a row of flowers in planter boxes.

"Look at the pretty flowers." Deborah pointed to the small purple and yellow flowers. "Maybe we should get *Dat* to make some planters. It would give him something to do."

"Jah, keep him out of our way." Emily giggled.

As soon as the door opened they were faced with Mrs. Cramer's smiling round face as she wiped her hands on a tea towel. "Come in girls. Luke and his *vadder* aren't here yet, but they shouldn't be long."

Emily walked through the doorway first and handed Mrs. Cramer the pie. "We brought you an apple pie. We were going to bring cake but since you only just got one yourself we thought an apple pie might be better. We thought you could have it tonight, or something."

"You girls didn't have to do that. How thoughtful. Come through to the kitchen."

They followed her through to the kitchen where a large table that would comfortably fit sixteen people took up the center of the room.

"This table's *wunderbaar,"* Deborah said running her fingers along the grain. "Was this made out of one piece of wood?"

"Jah. My *grossdaddi* made it when my *vadder* was only a young *bu.* I don't know what kind of wood it is, but it's certainly a good size."

"I don't think I've ever been into your kitchen before, Mrs. Cramer," Emily said.

The rattling of a wagon caused Mrs. Cramer to look out the window of the kitchen. "That will be Luke and his *vadder* now. Sit down, girls."

The girls pulled out their chairs and sat at the long table. The places had been set to one end of the table, the end closest to the kitchen. Emily was a little disappointed that they hadn't had much time to talk to Mrs. Cramer before Luke and his father had arrived.

"Can I do anything to help, Mrs. Cramer?" Emily asked half rising out of her chair.

"Nee, you just sit. I made us soup and bread. I hope that's all right for the both of you? It's chicken

47

and vegetable soup."

"That sounds lovely and smells delicious," Deborah said, even though the house smelled like cabbage –her least favorite food.

Seconds later, the back door opened and Luke and his father walked in. They both took their hats off and hung them on pegs just inside the back door.

Mr. Cramer saw them and said, *"Ach,* it's the Kauffman girls."

Deborah did not correct him. She was now a King, since that was Caleb's last name, and she saw no reason to go back to using her maiden name of Kauffman.

Luke passed his father with a huge smile on his face. "Hello, Emily, and Deborah. It's nice to see you both again."

"Jah, it's *gut* to see both of you," Mr. Cramer said before he looked at his wife. "And is that chicken soup I smell?"

Mrs. Cramer smiled. *"Jah,* I made it just how you like it, with lots of cabbage." She immediately looked at Deborah. "I didn't stop to think about you. Are you all right to eat cabbage?"

"I can eat anything," Deborah said.

"Gut." Mrs. Cramer turned back to the stove and ladled the soup out of the large pot into a smaller one for the table while Mr. Cramer sat at the end of the table.

"I'll help you with that, *Mamm,"* Luke said, and then carried the large white tureen to the table.

After Luke and his mother were seated, everyone closed their eyes to give thanks for the food.

"Would you girls like me to serve you, or would you like to serve yourselves?" Mrs. Cramer asked.

Luke stood up. "I'll serve everyone."

While Luke took all the bowls in turn and filled them, Emily had a chance to study him. He was tall, thick set, and reasonable to look at – not handsome, but not ugly. His hair was brown, the same color as his eyes. The things, which detracted mostly from his appearance, were three large moles on the left side of his face.

As Luke passed her a full bowl of soup, he

smiled at her. It was then that she noticed he had perfect white teeth, which made him almost pass as handsome. She returned his smile before she gave a sideways glance at her sister to see if she also had noticed these things about him. Deborah seemed more interested in staring into her soup, and Emily knew that was because Deborah had never liked cabbage, but Deborah would keep quiet and eat it to be polite. Their father had been extra careful about raising them to have good manners since he'd had to do the job of both mother and father.

"And what brings you girls by today?" Mr. Cramer asked.

At lightening speed Emily had an answer. "We felt like visiting before cold weather sets in."

"That's a nice surprise isn't it, Luke?" his father asked him.

Emily was embarrassed for Luke.

"Jah. It's lovely to see you girls."

"And how are the apples growing this year?" Deborah asked.

Luke opened his mouth to speak but his father

talked over the top of him. "Looks like we're going to have more than ever this year. We're heading for a bumper crop."

Luke nodded and was left with nothing to say.

Emily wondered what she could talk about so Luke could answer instead of his father. "And you're going to stay on here forever, Luke?"

"Where else would he go, Emily? The orchard will be left to him and solely him."

It was then that Emily knew Mr. Cramer thought she was there because she liked Luke. That made things very awkward. "That's nice," was all she could say as a response. She glanced over at Deborah hoping she would find something to talk about.

"I hear there's a barnraising soon?" Deborah said.

Luke jumped in as quick as a flash and said, "*Jah,* the Monday after next at Philip Lewis's farm. His barn got burned down, but you probably know about that."

Emily said, "*Nee* we don't know anything about

that. Can you tell us about it, Luke?"

"It was burned down by *Englisher* boys. The police caught them."

"That's dreadful! Were there any animals hurt?" Emily asked.

"Nee," Mr. Cramer interrupted. "The pigs and horses were in the barn but they managed to get them out in time. They lost a good deal of grain, but none of the animals were harmed."

Luke started to explain that some of the barn was left standing, and then his father finished his sentence for him.

"Jah, but everyone thought it would be best to pull the barn down and start anew."

"That's often best," Mrs. Cramer agreed.

"Will you girls be at the barnraising?" Mr. Cramer asked.

"Jah, we plan on going," Emily said.

After they finished the soup and then the cake, the men left to continue working in the orchard leaving the three women at the table.

"They seem like such hard workers," Emily said.

"*Jah,* they are. They're always thinking about ways to improve production even when they're here at home. The orchard's on their minds constantly."

"I imagine they would be thinking about it all the time," Deborah said as she stood to gather the dishes off the table.

Chapter 7

But seek ye first the kingdom of God,
and his righteousness;
and all these things shall be added unto you.
Matthew 6:33

"You don't have to help me here. You two go into the living room and I'll bring you a hot cup of tea," Mrs. Cramer said.

"*Nee*, Mrs. Cramer. Why don't you sit while we clean up?" Emily asked.

"I couldn't possibly. It's not right for you girls to clean my kitchen."

"We don't mind, we work well together and we're fast at it," Deborah said. "Why don't you sit back down and tell us about Luke?"

Deborah saying that was surely going to make Mrs. Cramer think that one of them was interested in her son. Emily didn't want Mrs. Cramer to get her hopes up that her son would finally find a wife.

"All right. You girls sure you don't mind?"

"Quite sure," Emily answered.

Mrs. Cramer grinned widely as she sat down. "And what would you like to know about him?"

Deborah began, "It's always amazed me how Luke has remained unmarried after all this time. He's nearly thirty, isn't he?"

"Nearly twenty nine. Twenty nine next month."

"Has he ever been close to marrying?" Emily asked.

"Nee."

"So he hasn't liked anybody in the last few years?

Mrs. Cramer thought for a while. "I'm sure he has but he doesn't tell his mother everything you know."

"If he were seriously interested in someone you would know that, wouldn't you?" Emily asked.

"I'll ask you girls right out. I'm too old to ask any other way. Do one of you girls like Luke?"

The girls looked at one another.

Mrs. Cramer added, "I won't say anything to anyone. I can keep a secret."

Deborah turned back to the kitchen sink. "I'm not considering anybody at all." She put a hand on her stomach. "Not in my condition and not so soon after my husband just died."

"I'm sorry, Deborah, I didn't mean to be cruel. Of course, it wouldn't be you. Pay me no my mind. I'm just a silly old lady. What about you, Emily?"

"You're not silly or that old, Mrs. Cramer," Emily said with a laugh. "It's just that my *schweschder* and I aren't looking for a man to marry."

Mrs. Kramer frowned. "You're not?"

Deborah shook her head and turned back to the kitchen sink while Emily sat down in front of Mrs. Kramer. "Are you sure you haven't noticed that Luke likes anybody? Does he look at someone a lot? Or does he talk to someone a lot?"

"Not that I've noticed. I do have a friend, Marie Oleff who has a *dochder*, Mary Lou. Mary Lou wants to get married. I've been meaning to have her over here to the house, but I don't want Luke to think I'm interfering in his life. If he thinks I want him to marry Mary Lou he won't like her for certain."

"Mrs. Cramer, I must confess that's why we're here. We thought we'd match Luke with a nice woman. I don't know why he's still single."

Mrs. Cramer smiled. *"Denke.* You girls are an answer to my prayers."

"And we've met Mary Lou at weddings," Emily said.

"I think I remember her," Deborah added. "She's a tall girl with dark hair, and she's very skinny? And she stays by her *mudder?"*

"Jah, that's her," Mrs. Cramer said. "Do you think you could both help to find some way for them to spend time together?"

"We can do that, can't we, Deborah?"

"Jah."

"I do have concerns that Luke will think she's too homely for him. She's a very plain looking girl."

"And Luke would be concerned about things like that?" Emily asked.

"I think that's a consideration to any young man

whether they'll admit it or not."

"She seemed okay to me," Emily said.

"She's really quite a nice girl," Mrs. Cramer insisted. "Would you put the pot on to boil, Emily?"

Emily giggled. "I totally forgot."

"Why don't I invite Mary Lou to the barnraising?" Mrs. Cramer asked. "You two can befriend her and invite her somewhere where Luke will be."

Emily spun around after lighting the stove. "That would be perfect, Mrs. Cramer. And we'll make sure that they talk to each other."

"You two have brightened my day. His *vadder* tells Luke all the time that he's just too quiet and needs to speak up."

Emily sat down again. "I don't think he's too quiet. He said enough today to keep the conversation going. Maybe he's not quiet at all."

"You girls would know better than I would about that kind of thing."

"What do you know about Mary Lou?" Emily asked.

"She's a simple girl and I like her. She keeps

bees and sells the honey from her *haus*. I'll give you girls a bottle each before you go. Whenever I visit they give me a bottle and now I've got about ten bottles. I don't use it that quickly."

"Denke. And how old is Mary Lou?"

"Around twenty five."

"Do you know why she's never married?"

"She seems happy to keep her bees and stay at home. That's all I know. She doesn't seem to have many friends."

"I've never met anyone that keeps bees," Deborah said.

Mrs. Cramer raised her eyebrows. "Haven't you? Old Arthur keeps bees. Well, he used to before he got too old."

"I didn't know."

"Mary Lou's hives are surprisingly close to their *haus*. When I last visited them they were having problems with the nearby farmers complaining that the bees were coming around their water and bothering their livestock. Mary Lou said they couldn't have been her bees because she had enough water out for them. That's when they had a falling out with their neighbors."

"That's not good," Emily said. "So she's quiet, stays at home, and likes to look after her bees?"

"That's right."

Deborah wiped her hands on a tea towel and turned around. "Emily, the pot's boiling."

Emily got up to make the tea. "What's the reason you think that your son and Mary Lou would be good together?"

"They're two lonely souls and they're both quiet. She's a lovely girl when you get to know her."

After they drank tea and cleaned up, the girls left Mrs. Cramer's house pleased that she was helping them match Luke with a girl. Now all they had to do was befriend Mary Lou. Firstly Emily wanted to get to know Luke a little better to make sure that Mary Lou was a good match. Just because they were both quiet didn't mean a thing.

"It's funny how Mrs. Cramer's helping match her son," Deborah said. "I can see why you like doing this and I think you're right about it helping people."

"Denke, Deborah. I'm glad one member of the *familye* can see that."

"How do we know that Mary Lou will be right for him?"

"We won't know at all until we see them together. We must hope Mary Lou can tear herself away from her bees to come to the barnraising." Emily stared down at the two bottles of honey in her hands while Deborah drove the buggy.

"Do you think Luke is handsome?" Deborah asked.

"I think he is, in a way."

"When he's married, his beard will cover those three large moles on the side of his face."

"Jah, that might make a big difference, but if someone falls in love with him his looks won't matter at all."

"That's just it, we've got to get someone to talk to him to see how nice he is."

"We? Does that mean you're going to help me, Deborah?"

Deborah laughed. "Definitely not. This is something that you have to do by yourself."

Emily pouted. "It would be much easier if you help me."

Deborah glanced over at her sister. "I think Tom's right about you needing to find something to do with your time."

"It annoys me that he says that all the time. And anyway, don't side with him, then everybody will be against me."

"I'm not against you. I can't be; I've only got you and *Dat* left."

"Did you notice Luke's *vadder* kept talking over the top of him?"

"Jah, I did. It's no wonder he's quiet, he can't get a word in edgewise."

"They also treat him as though he's much younger than he is."

"I suppose that's because they've always treated him that way."

"One *gut* thing about Mary Lou is that she lives with her *mudder* too, so she'll know what it's like for him to live with his parents."

Deborah yawned. "I think I'll have to take a nap when we get home. All the excitement of the day has really taken it out of me."

"*Denke* for coming with me."

"Are you going to mention to Tom that we saw him today?"

Emily shrugged her shoulders. "Only if it comes up in the conversation over dinner."

"We didn't invite Luke over for dinner like we'd planned."

Emily sighed. "I wanted to, but it was hard in front of his parents. They would've wondered why they weren't being invited too. And it would've been rude to invite Luke in front of them, don't you think?"

"*Jah,* I totally agree. If only we could have spoken to him on his own."

Chapter 8

Take my yoke upon you, and learn of me; for I am meek and lowly in heart: and ye shall find rest unto your souls.
Matthew 11:29

"Dinner's ready," Emily called to everyone. Tom and Mr. Kauffman walked into the room.

"Where's Deborah?" her father asked.

"She's upstairs having a little sleep; she got really tired when we went out today. Can you go and get her, *Dat*, while I finish a few things here?"

"Okay." Her father walked upstairs leaving Emily and Tom alone.

"How did you get along with your wicked plan today?"

Emily turned around from dishing potatoes into a bowl. "Wicked plan?"

"Your plan involving Luke. Do you have any other wicked plans apart from that one?"

Since Tom was being so mean to her, Emily decided not to tell him that she'd changed her mind about Deborah and Tom being a good match. "Oh, that plan. It went quite well. Luke and Deborah got on great together. And another thing, he's very talkative when he's not in a large group of people." Tom didn't need to know every detail of her schemes. She'd keep Mary Lou up her sleeve for the moment.

"Really?"

Emily nodded.

"Your *vadder* told me you went to the Cramers' place today."

"I figured he would've told you."

"And how long do you think it will take to match the two of them together? I can't imagine that Deborah is going to jump into another marriage so soon after Caleb's just gone."

"It could be the best thing for her."

"And you really think that Luke is a good choice for her? Assuming that she wants to marry again?"

"*Jah,* I do."

Tom shook his head. "I really don't see them together, at all. Have you told Deborah what you're trying to do yet? I think she should know."

"*Nee* if I tell her that might ruin everything. She just needs some time to see what a good man Luke is. She knows I'm trying to match him with someone, but that's all she needs to know for now."

"I told you before, he's the opposite of Caleb."

"I hardly think you'd know what's best for my *schweschder*. And besides, have you had any success in matchmaking?"

"Is not the kind of thing I would do."

"Exactly! You have none and I have two successes. And how many do you have again? None, didn't you say?" Emily leaned towards him and held out her ear.

"One day you'll go too far."

"That's your opinion, Tom; simply your opinion. And if you make any mess in the living room tonight with all those splinters over the floor, you're going to be the one to clean it up."

He grinned. "Your *vadder* and I never make a

mess."

Emily put the last of the bowls in the center of the table and sat down to wait for her father and Deborah. "They're taking a long time. The food's getting cold."

"Deborah is probably telling your *vadder* about how you were pushing her together with Luke today."

Emily leaned across and slapped him on his arm. "I did no such thing. I don't force people together; I just arrange for them to be close and the rest happens by itself. And speaking of matching people, now I know why you didn't want me to match you up."

He drew his eyebrows together. "What are you talking about?"

"I'm talking about Ruth. I saw you with her today."

"So that means I'm going to marry her?" Tom smiled broadly.

"*Nee.* It's just that I haven't seen you with a woman before."

He pulled a face. "I have women friends, which is just what Ruth is – a friend."

"Really? Does she know that?"

"Of course, she knows she's my friend."

"But is she hoping for something more?" Emily tilted her head to one side.

"I hardly think she'd have reason to."

"She's old and has never married." Emily heard Deborah walking down the stairs. "Shh. Don't say anything about Luke in front of Deborah."

As always, Tom shook his head at Emily.

Deborah walked into the room in front of her father. "Again you both stopped talking when I entered the room. Did I interrupt a private conversation?"

Tom leaned back in his chair, folded his arms and looked up at Deborah. "Seems your *schweschder* is intrigued that I spent some time with Ruth today. I'm not sure why."

Deborah giggled as she took her seat. "Emily gets curious about a lot of things. She usually means no harm."

Tom laughed.

Emily pursed her lips, and turned to her father. "Do you hear how they're talking about me, *Dat?*"

"You do bring it on yourself with that wild imagination of yours. Now let's say our thanks to the Lord for blessing us abundantly with this food."

They all bowed their heads and silently gave thanks.

When they had finished, Emily took a helping of beans. "You're all the same. No one in this *familye* has my vision or expertise in certain fields."

Tom and Deborah exchanged smiles.

"This looks good, girls," their father said.

"Emily did most of it while I took a nap. We had a big day of visiting people and we even went to your store, Tom. It's looking good."

"Denke. It was a struggle for the first few years but now it's going strong. You should have waited until I got back. Harold told me I only missed you by minutes."

Deborah looked over at Emily and caught her eye. "We were in a bit of a hurry, Tom," Deborah added.

"I guess you were in a hurry to go and see Luke?"

"*Jah* we had the midday meal with Luke and his parents," Deborah said.

"And how was that? Pleasant was it?" Tom asked.

"*Jah* Emily and I got to know Luke a little better. He's not as quiet as people say. That's what Emily and I think."

Tom looked over at Mr. Kauffman. "And what do you think of your *dochder* trying to match Luke now? It seems that Luke is the next victim on her agenda."

Her father fixed beady eyes on Emily. "Is that what you're doing?"

Emily took a deep breath. "Tom makes it sound like a bad thing, and it's not. It seems that Luke is being overlooked by the women in the community and there's nothing wrong with him."

Mr. Kauffman shrugged. "I think you're right, Emily. There's no doubt Luke has been overlooked, his younger brothers have all married."

Tom put his fork down on his plate. "If you ask me there's a good reason he's still living with his parents." He looked directly at Emily. "Did you ever stop to think that he might not want to get married?"

"Don't be ridiculous, Tom. Of course he wants to get married. Why wouldn't he?"

"Maybe to live a peaceful life?"

Mr. Kauffman smiled at Tom's comments and Emily glanced over to see her father's face.

"Don't laugh at him, *Dat*. You're only encouraging him to tease me."

"I didn't laugh at him, but he might have a point."

"And what point is that? Do you think Luke would rather be living with his parents by the time he's thirty or in his own home with his own *familye?*"

"And who do you think you will match him with?" Mr. Kauffman asked.

"There are a few women in the community I can think of; about five without thinking too hard."

When Tom coughed Emily knew he only did so

to hide a chuckle. She glared at him.

"Maybe we're being too hard on Emily," her father said.

Tom shook his head. "She forced two couples to spend time with each other and then they happened to think that they should get married. That doesn't mean that she should create a full-time career out of this."

The girls' father nodded. "Tom's right about one thing, Emily, there are better ways you could spend your time."

"I don't know how you can both say that. Don't you see how helpful I'm being to people? I'm doing a good thing. You can see that, can't you, Deborah? You said so just today."

"*Jah,* I do think that Emily is helping people. As long as the couples involve want to be married and want to find someone, I don't see anything wrong with that at all."

Tom raised a hand in the air. "Exactly right! As long as the people involved want it. You can't force these things on people, Emily."

"I've never forced anybody, Tom. And when does this have anything to do with you? You're not my *vadder* even though you act like it most of the time."

"Emily!" Her father glared at her from underneath his bushy brows. He was shocked at what she'd said to Tom.

Emily's gaze fell to her plate.

Mr. Kauffman wasn't finished there. "Just because you matched two couples together do you think you might have let pride creep in?"

"I'm not being prideful, *Dat.* I'm just happy that two couples are now together. It makes me happy."

* * *

Deborah said, "I think what Tom and *Dat* are concerned about is that you might cross over what someone wants for themselves. You wouldn't try to match people who don't want to be matched, would you?"

"And why wouldn't anybody want to be matched?"

"That something that's simply none of your business," Tom said. "You could be sticking your nose in where it's unwanted."

"I'm not," Emily said a little quieter now.

Deborah could see that Emily was getting upset because her bottom lip was trembling and her eyes were glistening and tears were about to fall. She had to come to her aid. "I think what Emily is doing is a good thing, and she'll make certain that the two people involve want to be matched, won't you, Emily?"

Emily nodded.

"I think you're right, Deborah. I don't see any harm in it if someone approached Emily and wanted her help," Mr. Kauffman said.

"Emily and I have a new project. Emily has been approached by someone for some help, and I am going to help her."

"If you're involved, I think it will be okay," Tom said to Deborah.

Emily glared at Tom. "You don't trust my judgment, Tom?"

Mr. Kauffman raised his hand. "Let's not have disagreements at the table."

Emily shook her head and remained silent looking down at the table.

Deborah said, "Is that a blueberry pie I see over there for dessert? Whenever did you get the time to make that, Emily?"

Tom took the hint. "You definitely are a *wunderbaar* cook, Emily."

Emily smiled. *"Denke,* Tom. I made the blueberry pie after you went to get some sleep, Deborah, and that's the last of our blueberries."

"We'll be sure to enjoy it," Mr. Kauffman said.

"And are you both doing your carving tonight?" Deborah looked at both Tom and her father.

"After we have a reading from the word of *Gott.* Are you girls going to join us for the reading?"

"Jah we will," Deborah said. "We'll leave the clearing up until after the reading."

"Okay," Emily said.

After they had their blueberry pie and cream, Emily did just what Deborah suggested and left all the dishes in the kitchen and sat down to listen to the Bible reading. Their father's favorites were the Psalms and he read out the whole of some sixty one. He closed his large Bible and looked over at his daughters. "This is just like old times."

"Deborah and I will do it more often," Emily said as she pulled Deborah to her feet. Deborah followed her back into the kitchen.

"Is everything okay? You don't seem like yourself tonight," Deborah said.

"I guess I do feel a bit out of sorts. I don't like it when everyone picks on me."

"Everyone was only giving their opinion. I'm sorry, I should've spoken up sooner."

Emily nodded. "And I don't know why Tom has to be so mean and bossy. He acts like he's our older *bruder.*"

"He's the kind of person who says what's on his mind even if he's going to offend someone. I don't think he'll change, and I think he likes teasing you as well."

"He does, I know that. Let's get these dishes done. Tomorrow I want to sew a new apron."

"That reminds me, I've got to make a new dress or two. I can't hide my bump any longer in the dresses I have." Deborah pulled her dress out to its maximum width across her stomach. "I've only got an inch left and then I'll be busting out."

"You've left it late, Deborah. You've only weeks to go."

"I know, I just had other things on my mind. Shall we go tomorrow and get some material?"

Emily nodded. "As long as *Dat's* not using the buggy."

While Emily filled the sink with soap and hot water, Deborah looked around the corner out into the living room and saw Tom and her father getting ready for their nightly wood whittling.

Chapter 9

Therefore being justified by faith,
we have peace with God through our
Lord Jesus Christ:
Romans 5:1

Later that same night, Emily stared at the living room with her hands on her hips. "What did the two of you have to say about this mess?"

Her father and Tom looked around the room.

Tom was the first to speak. "I said we'd clean it ourselves."

"I don't think I can wait for that to happen. It needs to be cleaned and it needs to be cleaned now."

"I suppose it's time we called it a night anyway, Tom."

"*Jah* it's getting late."

Emily walked back into the utility room just off from the kitchen and brought out a broom and dustpan.

"That broom's not big enough," Mr. Kauffman said.

Emily said, "The only other one we have is out in the barn."

"If you want Tom and me to do a proper job of it, you'll have to go out and get it," her father said to Emily before he turned to Tom. "Would you go out with her, Tom?"

"Okay." Tom lit one of the gas lanterns by the back door and led the way outside with Emily following close behind. Tom looked up at the sky. "It's a dark night tonight."

Emily looked up. "It's not so dark. I can see five stars and half of the moon."

Tom opened the barn door, flicked the main light on and placed the lantern just inside the door. He took a deep breath. "There's nothing like the smell of a barn."

Emily laughed. "What's nice about it?"

"Do you have to argue with me about everything?"

"I do, especially when you say strange things about a barn smelling nice."

Tom chuckled.

Emily continued, "It smells of hay and horse manure: I guess if you like horrible smells it would smell good to you."

Tom wandered over to the two horses and gave each one a pat on their neck. He turned around to look at Emily again and walked back to her "Now where's this broom your father was talking about?"

Emily looked round about her. "I can't see it anywhere. Maybe Deborah left it outside somewhere behind the *haus.*" When Emily saw that Tom was staring at her, she said, "What is it?"

"I'm just looking at how beautiful your eyes are in this light."

She shoved him on the chest with both hands. "Stop being stupid!"

He smiled. "I'm not being stupid. I'm just saying what I see."

"You can't say things like that."

He raised his eyebrows. "And why is that?"

Emily grunted and shook her head. "Just look for the broom so we can get back to the *haus.*"

"Or?"

"Or I'll stick you with that pitchfork over there." Emily pointed over to the corner of the barn.

Tom chuckled and went over to get the lantern where he'd left it. "I'll just have a look around to see if it might've been left in one of the stalls."

"I don't think Deborah would've left it there."

"It won't hurt to have a look while we're here."

Emily wanted nothing more than to get out of the barn in a hurry. Wanting to run back to the safety of the house, she stood in the doorway of the barn and waited for him.

"Nee I don't see it anywhere about. Looks like we're stuck with a smaller broom."

Emily took a step out of the barn as he walked closer. "That will teach you and *Dat* not to make a mess, then, won't it."

"It's not that much of a mess; most of it landed on the sheet. Here, you hold the lantern while I shut the barn door."

When she took the lantern from him he was too close for comfort. She was certain now that Tom liked her; she'd had suspicions before, but just now in the barn when he was talking about her eyes, she knew it was a fact.

After Tom locked the barn door, their hands touched as he took back the lantern. Emily was certain that he'd touched her hand deliberately. This would not do. They'd always been good friends, and he was a friend of the family. She didn't know what to think about how he'd spoken to her in the barn. They were silent all the way back to the house.

When they walked into the living room, her father was crouched over the dustpan and had already cleaned up the mess. He stood up straight when he saw them come into the room.

* * *

While Tom and Emily had been in the barn, Deborah helped her father clean the living room.

Deborah thought it a perfect opportunity to ask

her father a question or two. "I know we've never talked about this, *Dat,* but I often wondered why you never married again."

He took a while before he answered. "Sometimes you love someone so deeply it stays with you right here." He pressed his fingers just below his heart. "You girls might have benefited if I'd married again, but it wasn't to be. I know some people do get married again, but it wouldn't have been fair if I had. A woman deserves the whole attention and love of a man, and another woman would never have come close to your *mudder* in my heart. It's hard to put into words."

"I think I understand. You loved *Mamm* so much that she is still the only woman you have room for in your heart."

He nodded. "Did I ever tell you that your *grossdaddi* was married before he married your *grossmammi?*"

"Nee! Mammi wasn't his first *fraa?"*

He shook his head. "He was married when he was nineteen and they were together exactly one year before she drowned. Eight years later, he married your *grossmammi.*"

"*Dat,* why didn't you ever tell me?"

He made a growling noise in his throat. "Never thought to tell you."

"I would've liked to have talked to him about it while he was still alive. Do you know how *Mammi* felt about being his second *fraa?*"

"That's just the way it was, and she never knew any different."

"They seemed to be really in love from what I can recall."

"They were, they were devoted to each other."

"I wonder how things were between him and his first wife," Deborah said.

"I was curious about that and asked him. He said that he loved his first wife just as much even though both women were very different."

Deborah looked into the crackling fire. "I couldn't ever love anyone as much as Caleb."

"And that's how I felt about your *mudder.*"

"Did you ever get lonely, *Dat?*"

"I kept myself busy." He gave a chuckle. "The first few years, I used to talk with her as though she were still here."

Deborah saw her father's eyes glaze over and she wondered if he might cry. She was pleased that he was being so open with her, because he normally never talked about himself. *"Denke* for telling me these things, *Dat."*

He nodded, unable to speak for a moment.

There were so many more things Deborah wanted to ask, like if he'd ever been interested in another woman, but she couldn't, not when he was so upset. She'd heard that things get easier over time after you lose a spouse but things didn't look as though they'd gotten easier for her father. He still seemed very upset about the passing of his wife even though it had been so many years ago.

"We'll see them again, Deborah."

Deborah nodded. "I know he will, *Dat."* She'd never talked to her father about how much she'd missed her mother when she'd been growing up. That was something that she and Emily had talked often about between themselves but never to their father. Even though he had done everything he could for them, there was still the gap that only a mother could fill. Even to this day, as a grown woman, there was still the gap in her life that only her mother could fill.

"I'm going to bed. Let Emily think you cleaned the mess up, *Dat.*"

Her father laughed. "I will, as long as she doesn't ask if you helped."

* * *

"Well what do you think?" Mr. Kauffman asked Emily when she walked back into the living room with Tom. "Does the room pass your high standards, Emily?"

Emily placed her hands on her hips and walked over the room inspecting every corner. "Yeah, *Dat,* you did a fine job. I didn't know you could clean like this."

Her father laughed. "I had to do something to get me and Tom out of trouble."

"What did I do?" Tom asked.

Emily glared at him and shook her head. "I'm going to bed." She walked away leaving her father and Tom standing staring after her. She heard them both say good night and she nodded to them. When she got upstairs into the safety of her bedroom, she closed the door behind her and leaned against it. Shutting her eyes tightly, she thought back to what had happened in the barn. She'd felt new feelings for Tom in the barn when he looked into her eyes and spoke softly. *This is Tom, this is only Tom,* she reminded herself when she opened her eyes.

She walked over to the bed while untying the strings of her prayer *kapp.* After she tossed it onto her bed, she changed into her nightgown and slipped between the covers of her bed. Any other night she would've brushed out her long hair but tonight she would sleep with it braided.

Her hand covered her fast-beating heart while she wondered what life would be like if she and

Tom married. Is that why he had never allowed her to match him with another woman; because he liked her? And if that were true why had he never done, or said, anything about it? After imagining what it would be like to be married to Tom, Emily decided it was something that she couldn't think about. Who would look after her father every day? Her sister wouldn't have time to look after their father properly and be looking after her baby at the same time.

Maybe if she found Tom another woman; that would take his attention off her. She decided that's what she'd have to do; find a woman for Tom, a woman who wouldn't mind him spending so much time with her father.

* * *

After Deborah had helped her father clean up, she walked up the stairs. Tom and Emily had taken their time in the barn and Deborah wondered why.

The stillness of the night without being surrounded by constant chatter was something Deborah was looking forward to. She kicked off her shoes, pulled off her prayer *kapp,* and then unbraided her hair. As she brushed her hair, she remembered how much Caleb had liked watching her do just that every single night, even after the illness had set in.

Her baby kicked hard and she looked down and smiled. "You decide to wake up just when I'm ready to go to sleep." Deborah hoped that wasn't a pattern that would continue after the baby was born.

When she'd married Caleb, she'd had no idea that he was going to get so sick. Nor did she know her life was going to turn out to cause her so much heartache and pain. The more she thought about Caleb the more upset she got. The best solution that she'd found was to do something, anything that would take her mind off him. Nights were when the true loneliness set in. To keep her mind off Caleb, she concentrated on the trip to town that she was going to take with Emily the next day. She wondered what color dresses to make, and she fell asleep concentrating on different colors – anything to keep her from missing Caleb.

Chapter 10

*Whom having not seen, ye love; in whom, though now
ye see him not,
yet believing, ye rejoice with joy unspeakable
and full of glory:*
1 Peter 1:8

On their buggy ride into town, Emily said, "I'm going to stop in at Tom's store and ask if he can visit Luke to ask him to come for dinner."

"Really? Do you think that would be a good idea? It seems a little odd for him to ask on our behalf especially since he doesn't live at our house."

"Well he just about does. He's there every day."

"Well, Luke doesn't know that. I thought we were just going to wait for the barnraising and find out more about Mary Lou."

"I think we should talk to Luke and really get to know him a little bit better."

"Anyway, it'll be a welcome change for him rather than having dinner at home every night,"

Emily said.

"We have dinner at home every night."

"We've got each other and he's not got anybody except his parents who treat him like a child. *Dat* doesn't treat us like that."

"Alright, ask Tom if he'll do it. I like having people for the evening meal. Can we just go by the material store first, though? Sometimes I get a little tired and my brain gets a little fuzzy; I want to be thinking straight when I buy the material."

Emily agreed and then changed the topic of conversation back to Tom. "Did you see how funny Tom was when I asked him about Ruth?"

"I don't think he acted funny at all. He said that Ruth was just a friend."

Emily shook her head. "It was the way he said it. I do know him better than you. You've been out of the house for years when you were married and you've only been back no longer than a year."

"I suppose that's true. And since you know him so well, why is he acting funny at the mention of Ruth's name?"

"No other reason except that he likes her."

"And you're upset about that?" Deborah asked.

"I'm only upset because he insists he doesn't want to get married."

"Maybe he doesn't. Do you think that he is a liar?"

"*Nee*, but what if he doesn't know that he likes Ruth?"

Deborah sighed. "Can we have one day without talking about matchmaking?"

"*Jah* but not today. Can we do that tomorrow? I do have to ask Tom to invite Luke for dinner."

"And then can we be done with matchmaking talk for the rest of the day?"

"If that's what you want."

"I do." Deborah looked out the buggy at the stores they were passing. Everywhere she looked were cafes and restaurants. "Would you mind if we stopped for a bite to eat before we go and look at the material?"

"You hungry again?"

Deborah nodded. "I have to eat a lot for the

boppli."

"Do you want me to stop here?"

"Jah."

"Okay, there's buggy parking up here, and then we can walk back. I don't know how you can eat so much. I couldn't possibly fit another thing in."

"Good, all the more for me." Deborah laughed.

"Are you okay to walk back?

"A little walking is supposed to be good for me, so the midwife says."

After the buggy was secure, the two girls headed down the pavement. Deborah was so hungry she stopped at the first café they came to. "This one looks good."

"Okay. It looks just the same as all the others we passed in the buggy, but it's your choice."

Deborah pushed the glass doors open and headed to an empty table. As soon as she sat, she picked up the menu.

"What do you feel like?" Emily asked, following Deborah's eyes scanning the menu.

"Bacon and eggs." She folded the menu and

placed it back on the table. After Deborah gave the order to the waitress, she said, "I've been meaning to ask you something."

Emily scrunched up her nose. "What?"

Deborah gave a little laugh. "I happened to notice that you and Tom took a long time to find that broom in the barn last night."

Emily raised her eyebrows. "That's only because we couldn't find it; it was nowhere to be seen."

"No other reason?"

"What other reason could there be?"

Deborah smiled when she saw her sister was unable to look her in the eyes as she spoke. "*Nee* it's nothing."

"By the look on your face it is something. Don't tell me you think something's going on between me and Tom?"

Deborah said nothing and stared at Emily.

"Don't look at me like that, Deborah. If there were something going on, I'd tell you, but there's nothing between us."

"Did you ever wonder whether Tom might be

coming over to the *haus* for another reason other than to spend time with *Dat?*"

"*Nee* never. They both like to do that ridiculous carving or whatever it is that they do. They spend hours together and I'm not even in the same room, so he wouldn't be coming to see me; he's there to see *Dat.* Are you teasing me, or are you being serious? Because you're starting to worry me."

"You shouldn't be worried. What better man could there be for you than Tom?"

"He's far too old. He's a good seven years older. I'm certain he's thirty or thirty one."

"Well the older you get the less a seven-year age gap matters."

"What are you talking about?"

"Think about it. When he was eighteen you were seven, and that's far too big an age gap besides being seriously wrong for other reasons. When you were eighteen, he was …" Deborah counted up on her fingers. "He was twenty-five, and now you're twenty-four and he's thirty-one, and that seems an entirely reasonable age difference."

"He's closer in age to you, did you ever think of that?"

"He's interested in you." Deborah smiled.

Emily pulled her eyes away from Deborah's smiling face to look at the coffee the waitress had just placed before her. She glanced up and said, "Thank you," before the waitress hurried away. "You're not having *kaffe* today, Deborah?"

"Nee it's starting to make me feel a little bit sick to my tummy. I think I'll have to avoid it from now on."

* * *

Emily took a sip of coffee hoping that their conversation would continue in a different direction. What if Deborah was right and Tom did like her? It certainly seemed so, considering the words he'd spoken to her in the barn the previous night. "I'll get the sewing machine out today when we get home. We've got a lot to do, you've got your dresses, then there's my apron, and we better make a start on sewing for your *boppli."*

Deborah nodded. *"Jah.* We'll do that right after I make myself dresses. I don't want my big stomach to be too noticeable. It's best that I cover up. It won't take long to run up the dresses, or your apron."

The waitress brought Emily's breakfast over and placed it before her.

"This looks good, thank you," Deborah said to the waitress.

The waitress gave her a big smile back. "You're welcome. Would you like some cracked pepper with that?"

"No thank you."

After the waitress walked away, Emily silently watched Deborah eat, wondering what Deborah really thought about Tom.

"Mmm. This is *gut*. We should come here again," Deborah said.

"We've really got too much to do at home to spend too much time out and about. Since you've been home, I haven't really done the same amount of chores that I was doing before, and now everything is mounting up. The curtains need washing, the rugs need dusting, and so do the lights. And there are lots of other things that I can't think of right now."

Deborah finished chewing her mouthful. "I hope I haven't put you out of your routine. Sounds like I have."

"It's not your fault, it's mine. I just have to get back to keeping the place like I used to keep it."

"There's nothing to worry about, Emily, it looks fine. Besides, I'm here to help you with everything."

Emily nodded at what Deborah said while drumming her fingertips on the table. She looked around the crowded café at the people eating their breakfasts. Everywhere she looked were couples, men and women, except for one older lady sitting in the corner by herself. The lady was eating food from a plastic container that she must have brought with her, while steam rose from a cup of something in front of her. Since the woman had chosen to seat herself facing a blank wall, only her back was visible to Emily. She seemed lonely; maybe she was all alone.

Will I end up like that's when I'm her age - sad and alone? Dat can't live forever and when he goes home to be with Gott, I'll be all alone. Deborah's so pretty she'll surely have married someone else by then, and I don't want to be one of those sad maiden aunts who has to live with her relatives. I suppose I could stay in the haus by myself. She glanced up at the ceiling wondering whether Tom would come by and do repairs on the house, since by then, it would surely need many repairs.

"Why are you so quiet now, Emily? Are you thinking about Tom?"

Chapter 11

*Giving thanks always for all things unto God
and the Father in the name of our Lord Jesus Christ;*
Ephesians 5:20

As they sat in the café, Emily straightened her back and looked her sister in the eye. *"Nee.* I was not thinking about Tom."

Deborah giggled. "Who were you thinking about, then? You're never usually this quiet and I can nearly hear your brain ticking over about something."

Emily leaned in, and whispered, "I was just looking at that lady over there behind you, over your right shoulder. She looks lonely and she's eating out of that container. I was just feeling sorry for her because she looks sad and alone."

Deborah glanced over her shoulder at the lady. "She looks perfectly fine to me. She seems well-dressed and those shoes she's wearing can't have been cheap."

Impressed that her sister could sum all that up about a person in one glance, she took a second look at the lady. Her shoes were simple but elegant and could have been made out of fine leather unless it was just a good leather imitation. Maybe Deborah was right about the woman and perhaps she brought her own food because she was on a special diet.

"You can help me find a woman for Tom. I think your judgment about people is good. You had one glance at that woman and you summed her up pretty well."

Deborah laughed, and then wiped her mouth with a paper napkin. "And do you have Tom's permission for this? Don't forget what he said over dinner."

"I don't see why I need it. He's not the boss of me."

"He won't be happy if you mess about in his life. And no, I will not help you with that. I wouldn't be happy if you were trying to match me." Deborah popped the last morsel of food into her mouth.

When she placed both knife and fork side-by-side on the plate, should look straight into Emily's eyes. "What if he's in love with you?"

Emily forced a laugh. "Don't be silly."

"There's every possibility that it might be true."

"Don't say things like that, Deborah. I'll feel awkward around him if you keep saying things like that. It won't be good with him over at the *haus* all the time."

Deborah rose off her seat slightly and looked into Emily's coffee cup. "Are you finished?"

Emily drank the last mouthful. "I am now."

Deborah reached into her purse and placed the money for the food on the table.

"You're not going to leave it there, are you?"

"*Jah,* I always do. I know how much it was and I leave a little bit more too."

"Someone might walk past and take it."

Deborah leaned toward her. "Like who; that woman over there? I'd say that if we follow her we'd see her get into an expensive car."

Emily laughed, realizing her sister might be

right. She took the money up. "All the same, I'll go up and pay for it the way most people do."

Deborah stood. "Please yourself."

When they stepped out into the sunshine, Emily slipped her arm through Deborah's. "Come on. We'll go to Tom's store, and then we'll go and get the material."

"*Nee.* I thought we were going to do things the other way around."

"Really?" Emily would have preferred to go and see Tom right away. "Okay we'll do things your way. We can walk to the fabric store from here."

Once they were inside the store, they went their separate ways looking for fabric. Deborah called Emily over. "What do you think about this?"

Emily looked at the dark blue material. "It looks nice enough. Is it cotton?"

"It's some kind of a cotton blend. It seems tough. If you like it, I'll get enough for one dress."

"I like it."

"*Gut.* Now help me look for another color, but not a light one."

"Okay." Emily cast her eyes around about her. "How about this one?" she asked pulling out a length of a dark grape colored material.

Deborah felt the material between her thumb and forefinger. "I've never worn this color before, but it is a shade older ladies wear."

"You're not old, Deborah."

"I'm soon to be a *mudder* so I need to start acting like one. That starts with my dress."

"All right, then. Shall I take those two rolls up to the counter? I've already got the material at home for my apron. I just remembered I bought some a while back."

"Let me make the dresses first," she reminded Emily. "Otherwise I'll have nothing to wear soon." Deborah pulled her dress tight over her stomach.

"You're getting big. I won't say another word until you've made the dresses." Emily carried the two rolls of material over to the counter, pleased that Deborah was now thinking about getting things ready for the baby. She hadn't wanted to push her, but the closer the time got, the more she worried that Deborah wouldn't be prepared when the baby arrived. Now, it looked like Deborah was thinking more about her baby rather than dwelling on Caleb being gone.

"I think the *boppli* should be dressed all in white. What do you think?" Deborah asked when Emily walked back to stand beside her.

"That's a good choice. You're not going to sew everything, are you? You can buy the undershirts and t-shirts in that stretchy fabric, and they're so hard to sew."

"I know, that material slips all the time. Okay I'll buy that type of thing, and we'll make the other clothes."

The girls spent another hour in the fabric store choosing material. When they had made their selections and had them cut, they headed out of the store with two large bundles of fabric.

"This should keep us busy for quite a while," Deborah said.

"I'd say so."

"Now we can go and see Tom, if you'd like."

Emily laughed. "All right as long as you're not hungry again. We don't have to stop for you to eat again, do we?"

"I think I'll last until we get home. After we see Tom, I think we should stop somewhere and buy peanuts. Roasted peanuts in the shell."

"You're not having cravings, are you?"

"I think so. I was thinking about peanuts all day yesterday and I don't think I'll stop thinking about them until I eat some."

"Okay. Remind me, and we'll get them before we leave."

Chapter 12

And above all things have fervent charity among
yourselves:
for charity shall cover the multitude of sins.
1 Peter 4:8

Emily didn't know why but she found herself a little bit excited about seeing Tom in his store even though she saw him nearly every night. As soon as they entered his store, Tom saw them and walked over to them.

"This is a nice surprise. Have you come to look at cribs, Deborah?"

"*Nee,* Caleb's *schweschder* mentioned I could use one of hers, but it wouldn't hurt to look at some while I'm here."

He pointed to the far end of the store. "They're over that way. I'll show you."

"*Nee,* Deborah can look by herself while I ask you something," Emily insisted.

Deborah hurried away.

He looked confused and raised an eyebrow at Emily.

She took a deep breath, and began, "The reason we're here is that I have decided to ask you something."

Tom crossed his arms over his chest. "And what would that be?"

"You see, when we visited with Luke's family we had no time to talk properly with him and we couldn't invite him to dinner without inviting his parents. We didn't want to appear to be rude. I was hoping you would visit Luke and invite him to come for dinner?"

"You want me to ask him to dinner at your place? That's a little odd."

"*Nee,* not really. I don't think it is."

Deborah walked up to them and Tom looked at her. "Are you in on this too, Deborah?"

Deborah pulled a face. "I would like him to come to dinner. It would be nice to get to know Luke a little better. And I also think it would be good for him to have some time away from his parents."

"*Jah*, they are a little smothering," Tom said, appearing to be deep in thought.

"You think so too?" Emily asked.

He nodded.

Emily moved closer to him. "So you'll do it?"

"I suppose I will. Must it be done today?"

Emily nodded. "Today would be good."

He shook his head and looked at the floor, and muttered, "How did I know you were going to say that?"

When Deborah wandered away, Emily explained, "You see, I'm not really trying to match Deborah with Luke. Well, I was originally, but I saw that you were right, they aren't a *gut* match, but there might be someone else for him."

"So, you're more interested in matching Luke rather than finding someone for your *schweschder?*"

Emily waved a hand in the air. "She won't have trouble finding another husband, but Luke needs help finding a *fraa.*"

"Does he know this?"

Emily shrugged. "I don't know."

"And who is the lucky lady you have lined up for him this time?"

"Mary Lou."

"Okay … I don't know any Mary Lous."

"Neither do I, not very well anyway. I've met her at weddings. I happen to know that she'll be at the barnraising, so I have to get my plan ready by then."

He rolled his eyes. "Come on. Let's go and see what Deborah's looking at."

"Will you help?" Emily asked.

"If you're asking whether I'll ask Luke to your place for dinner, then the answer is yes. And for anything else the answer is no."

Emily was pleased that at least he'd agreed to ask Luke for dinner. She walked next to Tom as they wandered over to Deborah.

Tom put both hands on the crib Deborah was looking at. "Nice, but the one behind you is our most popular seller."

Deborah turned around to look at it. "It's lovely. How much is it?"

He pointed to the crib. "This crib, that dresser, and that title with the drawers –made to be used as a change table –they're all going to your place tonight."

"What do you mean?" Deborah asked.

"They are my gift to you, but the *boppli* is to call me *Onkel* Tom." He glanced over at Emily and winked at her.

"Tom, I can't let you do that, and, of course, my *boppli* would call you *Onkel* Tom."

"Well, that's settled, then. I'll bring them with me tonight."

"It's too much, Tom," Deborah said.

"Nee it's not. It's the least I can do. Your *vadder* and you two girls are my second *familye;* you have to allow me to do this."

Deborah put her fingertips over her mouth. "Are you certain?"

"I wouldn't have said so if I wasn't."

Emily stood next to Deborah and put her hand on her shoulder. "Now, don't cry. See what happens when you leave things until the last moment?"

"Denke, Tom. I'm not sure what to say to you. I'm very grateful. This means so much to me and the *boppli,* and Caleb would want to thank you as well."

Emily looked at Deborah's eyes and saw tears brimming. "Oh no. I better get you home now."

As they walked out of the store, Tom called after them, "I'll see you girls later tonight."

They turned and waved to him.

"What do you think of that, Emily? How generous is he? I feel embarrassed."

"You shouldn't feel embarrassed. You do nice things for everyone all the time, so you have to accept it when people do the same for you." Emily looked up at the gray sky as she felt raindrops fall on her bare arms. "It's going to rain."

"The buggy's not far."

"What about your peanuts? We can get them over there." She pointed to the farmers market.

"Jah, gut. We must get the peanuts."

Chapter 13

He that loveth not knoweth not God;
for God is love.
1 John 4:8

The girls walked in their front door with the peanuts and the bags of fabric under their arms.

"I suppose before I do anything else I'll have to fix up my room to make way for all the furniture Tom's bringing." Deborah had thought she'd get a hand-me-down crib; she'd never guessed she'd be able to have a brand new crib and other furniture too. "It was so generous of Tom."

Emily screwed up her nose. "It was, but he's here every night so I suppose he does feel like he's one of the *familye.* Let's have something to eat first, and then I'll help you move things around."

"Where's *Dat?*" Deborah asked just as they heard hammering coming from upstairs.

Both girls looked at each other.

"I wonder what he's trying to do now?" Deborah said.

Their father was always trying to fix things around the house and Tom was the one who had to undo all the things he'd tried to fix.

"I'll go and have a look." Emily placed her parcels down on the couch.

Deborah picked up the packet of peanuts and headed to the kitchen. She sat down at the table, and made a start on shelling the nuts. After she ate a few she was glad she'd listened to her cravings – they tasted great. She was onto her second handful when Emily came into the kitchen followed by their father.

"You never guess what I found *Dat* doing, Deborah."

Deborah looked up to see her father looking guilty. "What were you doing, *Dat?*" Emily spoke for him. "He found my old crib and he was trying to fix it up for you."

"Were you?"

Her father nodded. "I found it in the attic. I knew

your *mudder* and I didn't throw it out."

"You shouldn't go climbing around in the attic by yourself," Emily said. "I told *Dat* what Tom's bringing tonight."

Their father laughed. "Just as well too, because I broke it while I was trying to fix it. I don't think it's much good for anything now apart from firewood."

As Deborah cracked another peanut shell, she wondered how her father could break the crib that badly. "I'll go up and have a look at it. I don't think I've ever seen it before."

"You would've seen it when Emily was a *boppli.*"

"I don't remember it at all."

"Did you girls bring any food back with you?" He pulled out a chair and sat down at the table.

"Only peanuts," Deborah said pushing the bag of nuts over.

His mouth turned downward. "I don't eat them."

"I'll make us some lunch, *Dat,*" said Emily. "It'll only take fifteen minutes."

"Okay. I was looking forward to fixing that crib

up for you, Deborah."

"Denke, Dat. It would've been nice to use our old one."

* * *

While Deborah and her father talked at the kitchen table, Emily busied herself with fixing them something to eat. It would have to be cold cuts and salad, and they'd have a hot meal that night. Emily's mind was drawn back to Tom when they'd seen him earlier. He said he'd like the baby to call him *Onkel* Tom, and then he winked at her. Was that a hidden meaning? Did he mean that he hoped one day that she would marry him, and Deborah's baby would become his nephew or niece? Tom was nothing like the man that she saw herself with. Not that she'd had a clear picture of what that man would have to be like, but it wasn't Tom. Tom was just someone who'd always been in her life.

After lunch, Emily helped Deborah move some

things around in her room to make way for the new furniture. When they were through, they sat down on Deborah's bed staring at the old broken crib.

"It reminds me of *Mamm,*" Deborah said.

"It does. I wonder what she was like."

"I think she was kind and loving, like a *gut mudder.* I remember hanging on to her skirts. That must have been annoying, but she never pushed me away or said a cross word."

"It would be nice to have some memory of her like you do."

Deborah nodded. "That's all I can remember, that and her singing to me. What do we do with the crib? I don't want to throw it away, or use it for firewood."

"Perhaps Tom will have some ideas to make it into something else."

"I can't think what."

Emily shook her head. *"Nee,* neither can I."

"Just think that we were once that small that we fitted into that."

"I know. It was so long ago. I'll go downstairs

and get the sewing machine out."

"I'm a little tired to start the sewing today. Maybe tomorrow?"

"Okay. I'll get it out ready for tomorrow. Why don't you have a sleep and I'll start getting dinner ready?"

"*Denke*, Emily, you're such a *gut schweschder.*"

* * *

Deborah woke to the sound of a wagon rattling. That must be Tom. Out the window the afternoon sun was sinking in the sky. After she rubbed her eyes, she placed her prayer *kapp* back on and looked out the window. It was Tom with another man, and they had her baby furniture in the back of the wagon.

She went downstairs to see if she could help. When she reached the wagon, they were untying ropes.

"Deborah, you've met my *bruder* before, haven't

you?"

Deborah looked over at the man whom she'd assumed was one of Tom's employees. He was wearing plain blue jeans and a white shirt. She only knew of one brother Tom had, and he'd left the community many years ago to become a doctor. Tom had been joking when he'd asked if she'd met him before. "Of course, I remember your *bruder.* It's been a long time." He flashed a smile at her, and Deborah searched her mind for his name.

"Hello, Deborah." As if reading her mind, he said, "It's Nathan."

"Jah, Nathan. Hello." This man was every bit as handsome as Tom and she wondered if Emily had seen him. "Can I be of help?"

"Nee. We'll sort this out, but you can tell us where you want it when we get it inside."

"I'll wait inside, then." Hurrying inside to tell Emily about the handsome visitor, Deborah passed her father heading to the wagon. As soon as she walked into the kitchen, she saw Emily looking out the window.

Emily turned around to look at her. "Who's that?"

"Tom's *bruder.* He's a doctor. He left the community when he was only a teenager. You would've met him a long time ago."

"Is he coming back to the community?"

"I don't think so. I don't know anything, I just saw him here now. Tom hasn't spoken of him in years." Deborah walked over to the window and stood by her sister and they both stared at the man who'd become a stranger.

"He looks strong, like he's a farmer," Emily said. "I hope he can stay for dinner."

"Jah, we can find out more about him if he does. I'll ask him." When they saw that the men were now carrying the crib toward the house, Deborah said, "I better go and tell them where it needs to go."

Emily didn't answer; she was too busy staring at Nathan.

Upstairs, Deborah told them where she wanted everything.

On their way out to get the next piece of furniture, Tom looked at the old crib. "What's that?"

"When we got home, we found *Dat* up here trying to repair it. It's Emily's old crib."

Tom laughed and put his hands on the side of it rocking it to and fro. "I wouldn't like to put any *boppli* in this. What are you going to do with it?"

Nathan stood in the doorway looking at her, which made her nervous. "I don't like to throw it away. Emily and I thought you might be able to turn it into something else."

He frowned at her and tipped his head to one side. "Such as?"

Nathan stepped forward. "If you cut the front railings off it would make a nice baby chair. You'd have to lower the legs, and you could get a mattress, or a solid cushion made to fit."

"I like the sound of that. Could you do that Tom?"

Tom turned around and stared at his brother. "You stick to medicine."

Nathan smiled. "I keep telling you I'm good at

everything."

Tom looked back at Deborah. "I can do that for you as long as my big *bruder* helps me and shows me how to do it."

"I'd be delighted to try my hand at something like that again. We used to do woodwork as boys all the time," Nathan explained to Deborah. "Come on, Tom, before Mr. Kauffman starts unloading the wagon by himself."

"Can you stay for dinner, Nathan?"

Tom butted in, "He's in a hurry to go."

Nathan chuckled. "I'm in no rush. Don't mind him. Thank you, I'd love to stay for dinner."

Deborah followed them down the stairs to tell Emily the news that he was staying. When she reached the kitchen, Emily was staring out the window at them again.

"What would you do if they turned around and saw you?"

Emily looked over her shoulder at her sister. "You can't see in from outside, there are too many reflections. As long as we don't have the lights on inside."

"He's staying for dinner."

"He is?" Emily straightened her prayer *kapp,* and licked her lips. "I'm excited to find out all about him. I wonder why Tom never speaks about him." She looked outside again. "You better go now; they're bringing the dresser in."

"That's all right. I told them where everything needs to go. Now I can help you in here."

While the girls finished making the dinner, Tom, Nathan and Mr. Kauffman arranged the new furniture in Deborah's room.

Chapter 14

Be strong and of a good courage,
fear not, nor be afraid of them:
for the LORD thy God, he it is that doth go with thee;
he will not fail thee, nor forsake thee.
Deuteronomy 31:6

Over dinner, Tom announced, "You'll be pleased to know that I've visited Luke and he'd be only too happy to come to dinner on Friday."

"*Gut,* I'm so pleased," Emily said.

Tom turned to his brother, and said, "That's Luke Cramer. Do you remember him?"

"Yes, we went to school with him. What's he doing these days?"

"He's not married and these girls think he should be."

Nathan looked at both girls. "Why's that?"

"He's still living with his parents and all his younger brothers are married," Emily explained.

Nathan nodded and then looked at Deborah. "And what do you think about that, Deborah?"

Deborah shrugged her shoulders and smiled. "I'm not sure what I think about it."

Tom turned to Nathan and explained, "You see, Emily has a specialty which is matching people together. She's had two successes; she's got two couples married off already."

"I get it." Nathan looked down at his food.

"And what brings you here, Nathan? Are you just visiting Tom?" Deborah asked.

"I'm here for Tom's birthday."

Everyone looked at Tom.

"He's joking, that's next week. Birthdays aren't a big thing to me. Nathan's visiting me because he's missed me."

Nathan laughed.

"Will you have your birthday over here as you usually do?" Mr. Kauffman asked.

"If you'll have me, I'd like that, but that means you'll have to put up with Nathan again. That is, if you'll come here again for my birthday dinner,

130

Nathan?"

"Yes, I'd like to."

Emily giggled loudly and Deborah looked over at her. Could Emily be nervous? It seemed so.

Mr. Kauffman laughed as well. "We'll have anyone you'd like to invite, Tom. Including your long lost *bruder*. When is your birthday again, Tom?"

"Tuesday."

"That's only five days away," Emily said. "I can think of a couple of people that I'd like to invite as well."

"You're not going to use my birthday dinner to match anyone up, are you? I thought you were going to do that at the barnraising."

Emily pouted. "I might do it at both places. The barnraising's Monday and your birthday is Tuesday. If all goes well, I might have two extra people to invite to your birthday, Tom."

After dinner, everyone sat in the living room to talk. Tom, Mr. Kauffman and Emily were arguing about something and Nathan and Deborah were left out.

"I was very sorry to hear about Caleb, Deborah."

"Denke, Nathan."

"When is your baby due?"

"I've got about three weeks to go. And you're a doctor now, Nathan?"

"Yes, I'm working at one of the local hospitals. Didn't Tom tell you? I thought my brother would've been boasting of all my achievements."

"You know we don't boast of anything, Nathan," Mr. Kauffman said.

Nathan smiled as he looked over at Mr. Kauffman. "I know; I do remember that."

Emily said, "I think he was only joking, Dat."

Mr. Kauffman chuckled. "I didn't realize that."

"I don't tell anyone about you because I've got better things to talk about than you." Tom joked to his brother.

"Why don't we have *kaffe,* girls?" Mr. Kauffman suggested.

When the girls went into the kitchen, Deborah said, "He's certainly changed a lot."

"You remember him. I don't, but then again, Tom wasn't spending so much time here at the house back then."

"That's true."

"Don't you think he's handsome, Deborah?"

"Jah, of course, don't you?"

Emily nodded. "Do you think he might come back to the community?"

"Nee, I don't think so. It took him years to get where he is and I think he decided before he left that he'd never come back. He always spoke about becoming a doctor even as a *bu."*

Not long after they had coffee, Tom announced that he and Nathan would have to leave. His brother had an early start at the hospital the next day.

* * *

After breakfast the next morning, the girls began sewing. Deborah cut her first dress out on the kitchen table, and then tacked it loosely before sewing it on the diesel-powered machine. The sewing machine was on a small table at the back of the kitchen.

"Did you know that Tom has invited Nathan for dinner tonight too?" Emily asked.

"What? Nathan and Luke are coming on the same night?"

Emily nodded.

"I wonder how Luke will do with that. He's awfully shy," Deborah said.

"He's not that shy. I think it's just that his parents never let him speak."

"We'll see how he is at dinner tonight," Deborah said.

"Remember, we've got to find out as much about him as we can to see if Mary Lou is a good fit for him."

"I know, and then we talk to Mary Lou at the barnraising."

"That's right."

"I can see why you like matchmaking; it's kind of fun."

Emily giggled. "I'm glad you like it; it'll be *gut* to have a helper. You must say what you think the next time *Dat* and Tom are picking on me about the matchmaking."

"I know. I will. Should I stop sewing and start cooking dinner soon?"

"You don't have to help. I can do it on my own since it's still early in the day."

"Are you sure?"

Emily nodded and then looked over Deborah's shoulder. "Should you do little pleats on the shoulders, I mean the sleeves? I've seen that some women have that on their dresses."

"Nee, I just want it as plain as possible."

"Okay. I thought it might have been a nice change to have something a little different."

Deborah stopped sewing and stared straight ahead. "I wonder where Nathan lives and why he's coming here for dinner again tonight. He can't live too far away and he's never visited before."

"He might miss his little *bruder,* just as Tom said."

"If that were true he could visit him in his store since it's closer to the hospital."

Emily began cutting the vegetables for dinner. She'd decided on roasted chicken and a variety of vegetables, figuring that everyone liked chicken.

Chapter 15

By whom also we have access by faith into this
grace wherein we stand,
and rejoice in hope of the glory of God.
Romans 5:2-5

Luke was the first to arrive for the evening meal at the Kauffman's house. The girls saw him out of the kitchen window, and kept watching as their father went out to greet him.

"I thought Tom would be the first to arrive," Emily said.

"Me too. He's normally here before this."

"Maybe Nathan held him up. He could've had a big emergency at the hospital."

"I'll put everything in the bowls in the center of the table and cover them with lids. That'll keep it all nice and hot."

Emily frowned. "I hope Tom isn't going to be too late." She leaned out the window. "That's him now. I can see his buggy."

"Does he have Nathan with him?"

"Jah, I can see two people in the buggy so the other man must be Nathan."

"That's good, now dinner won't spoil."

They heard the front door open, and both girls stopped what they were doing to say hello to Luke.

Luke took off his hat and nodded hello to them. Mr. Kauffman took the hat from him and put it on one of the pegs by the front door.

"Will dinner be long, girls?" their father asked.

"We're ready to start as soon as everyone gets here."

"They are other people coming?" Luke asked.

Mr. Kauffman answered, *"Jah,* we've got Tom coming, and his *bruder,* Nathan."

"I haven't seen Nathan in a long time. He's a doctor now, isn't he? One of my *bruders* saw him in the hospital."

"Jah, he is," Emily said.

"Why don't we sit down until Tom comes in? We saw him coming up the road so he won't be long."

The two girls, Mr. Kauffman and Luke sat in the living room.

Everyone was silent until Emily said, "I'm looking forward to the barnraising."

"So am I," Luke said. "We haven't had one in a long time. Shame that the Wilson's barn burned down, though."

"It was a blessing that they didn't lose any livestock," Mr. Kauffman said.

Then Tom opened the door and walked in, with his brother following close behind. Tom never knocked on their door; he treated the place as his own.

Emily bounded to her feet. "Finally! Dinner would've been cold if you'd taken any longer. As it is, I can't be blamed if the dinner is lukewarm."

Tom stared at Emily. "Nathan had an emergency at the hospital and that's why we're late."

Emily's mouth fell open. "I'm sorry, Nathan. Don't mind me, I always talk first and then think later. An emergency is far more important than dinner."

Nathan laughed. "Don't listen to him, Emily. I didn't have an emergency, but I'm the one to blame for being late."

Emily frowned at Tom.

"I wasn't making things up, Emily. All things at the hospital are really emergencies."

Nathan frowned at his brother. "I don't think that's exactly true."

"That's a discussion for another time." Tom looked over at Luke. "Hello, Luke. Good to see you again. You remember Nathan?"

Luke stood and walked over to the brothers. "Yes, I do." He stretched out his hand to shake Nathan's."

After everyone had greeted each other, Deborah who was now standing beside Emily, said, "Everyone to the kitchen, then."

They all made their way to the kitchen.

"Tom and *Dat* you can sit in your usual places, and Luke you can sit beside Deborah." Emily had positioned Luke opposite her so she could more easily ask him questions.

Once they were all seated, they bowed their heads and said their silent prayers of thanks for the food. Emily was the first to open her eyes and then when all eyes opened, she stood and took off the covers from the bowls in the center of the table.

"Everyone help yourselves," Deborah said.

"Before you and Nathan arrived, Tom, we were talking about the barnraising," Mr. Kauffman explained.

"Ah yes, the barnraisings. They're a lot of hard work," Nathan said.

"I think being a doctor would be a lot of hard work too, Nathan," Emily said.

"That's true, but a different kind of work."

"What sort of doctor are you Nathan? Do you specialize in anything?" Luke asked.

"I specialize in ear, nose and throat."

"And how many years did it take you to study that?"

"There were four years of medical school and five years of residency. I see mostly children and young people. The bulk of the problems people have are hearing issues or tonsillitis. Many Amish people are afflicted with hearing loss, which is unfortunately inherited. So, from time to time I see people from the community."

"It must be good to help so many people," Emily said.

"It is very rewarding."

"There's no need to dominate the entire dinner conversation, Nathan. You always seem to do that," Tom joked.

"When people ask me a question, I generally answer it. It's not my fault," Nathan said with a laugh.

"Just be quiet and let others speak," Tom said before he turned to Luke. "Luke, you're welcome to come to my birthday dinner right here if you'd like to come. It's on the night after the barnraising."

Luke rubbed his jaw. "I'd like that, if that's okay with everybody?" He looked directly at Emily.

"*Jah* we were going to ask you, weren't we, Deborah?"

"We were. We'll have a few people here; it'll be

a nice night."

"And don't bring him any presents," Nathan said.

Tom laughed. *"Jah* please don't bring me any presents I'm far too old for gifts."

Mr. Kauffman sat quietly enjoying the conversation that was going on around him.

"I don't see you at any of the youth singings, Emily," Luke said.

"Do you still go to those, Luke?" Tom said before Emily could answer.

Nathan dug Tom in the ribs. "He wasn't talking to you he was talking to the young lady."

Emily raised her eyebrows. *"Nee* I don't go to them anymore." Emily thought that Tom was being a little rude. Especially since they were trying to boost Luke's confidence not destroy it.

Luke turned to Tom to explain, "I only go to the singings because I organize them. I enjoy doing that and being around the young people. They've got so much energy and vitality. We have people Emily's age come, and I thought she might enjoy a night at a singing every now and again."

Emily noticed that Tom seemed to resent Luke's presence at dinner. He wasn't being terribly friendly.

After dinner, everyone sat together in the living room.

While everyone was engaged in a conversation, Nathan turned to Deborah who was sitting next to him.

"Are you going to have a midwife for the birth, Deborah?"

"*Jah,* Molly Briggs, do you remember her?"

"I do. I didn't realize she'd still be around. She must be a fair age by now."

"She's had a lot of experience."

"I suppose that's true. Are you going to have your baby tested just in case…"

"Caleb's doctor has already booked me in. Before Caleb died the doctor knew we were having a baby. They still don't really know what was wrong with him."

"I know. Tom has told me a little about his

condition. It was in the sixties that they found the Amish have a high incidence of genetic problems. Many of them, they're still finding out about."

Deborah nodded and didn't want to talk about it. She didn't know how she'd cope if her child was sick.

* * *

When Luke left the Kauffman house, Emily found herself alone by the front door with Tom.

"What's the real reason you had Luke over here tonight, Emily?"

Emily stared up into Tom's face. Could he be jealous? "What makes you think it's for any other reason than the one I already told you?"

"I think you're treading on dangerous ground."

"In what way?"

"I think Luke has a crush on you."

Emily shook her head. *"Nee* I hardly think that's true."

"Didn't you see the way he kept looking at you and talking to you? He excluded everybody else."

"That's because you were being rude. You were being rude to Luke and your *bruder.*" Emily crossed her arms over her chest.

"I'm always rude to Nathan, he enjoys it. And how was I being rude to Luke?"

"You were making fun of him."

"I was not. That's just the way I talk; I like having a bit of fun, that's all. If your *vadder* had thought I was rude he would've said something."

Emily shook her head. *"Dat's* in a world of his own sometimes. I think you were picking on Luke."

"I wasn't. How could you say that?"

"Luke is very quiet and Deborah and I were trying to give him more confidence."

"And how were you doing that? Are you making him think that you like him, is that how you're trying to boost his confidence?"

Emily opened her mouth in shock. *"Nee!* That would be a horrible thing to do. I would never do that."

"Did you see the way he kept looking at you?"

"He wasn't looking at me in any particular way. You're being silly and now I'm getting angry with you."

Tom raised his eyebrows, and then he shook his head. "Are you certain it's Mary Lou you're going to match with Tom? Or do you think you might fancy him for yourself?"

"What kind of question is that, Tom? *Nee,* I don't like Luke in that way, or anybody else." Emily stood, and stomped back into the house.

Tom walked after her. "Wait, Emily. I'm sorry, that was a silly thing for me to say."

"That's all right. I'm just tired I guess. Normally all the things you say don't bother me."

When Tom and Emily turned around, they saw everyone else sitting silently in the living room. They walked over and joined them.

Tom said, "I'm going to bring a lot of food over for my birthday dinner. And I'm guessing it's probably best to do that the day before the barnraising because you won't have any time to tend to it the day of the barnraising and the morning of the party will be too late." He looked at Emily. "Is that correct?"

"Jah, that will be good, thank you Tom. What kind of food would you like me to cook you?"

"I'll see what's at the farmers market and you can choose the dishes yourself when you see the ingredients I bring. Will that suit you?"

"Okay."

"Denke, Emily. I do appreciate you going to all this trouble for me every birthday. It's really not necessary."

Emily smirked. "I'll remember that for next year."

Chapter 16

Blessed is the man that trusteth in the LORD,
and whose hope the LORD is.
Jeremiah 17:7

The morning of the barnraising, Emily and Deborah and their father pulled up in their buggy at the Wilsons' house right at seven in the morning. It was an early start for the workers, and the women were going to be just as busy as the men since they'd have to keep the food and drinks ready for the workers.

Not long after they'd arrived, they saw Mrs. Cramer pulling up in her buggy. They looked closer to see that she had Mrs. Oleff and Mary Lou with her.

"Let's go and meet them," Emily said, hurrying over to them.

Deborah nearly caught up with her sister and followed close behind. They reached the buggy just as Mary Lou was getting out. She was a tall girl, and plain looking. When Mary Lou smiled at them Deborah saw that her face lit up and she looked a different person – almost attractive.

"I'm glad you've come, Mary Lou. Would you like to stay by Deborah and me today?" Emily asked.

"Jah, I'd like that."

The three girls headed back to the Wilsons' house where the preparations for the food were underway. The men had already laid out trestle tables just outside the house, ready for all of the food.

During the day, Deborah had a chance to have another talk with Molly, the midwife. She had so many questions for her. Since the birth was so close, Molly was now making weekly visits to Deborah's house.

It was a long day, and the work was tiring for both men and women. Just as at all the barnraisings, the barn was mostly finished by the end of the day.

When many people had gone home, Emily spotted Tom and hurried over to him. "I've been talking to Mary Lou all day and I'm certain she's just the woman for Luke."

Tom wiped the sweat off his forehead with his sleeve. "Yeah? And why's that?"

"I can't explain everything to you. Some secrets are better left untold. You just have to trust me."

He leaned closer to her. "More importantly, why are you telling me?"

Emily took a step back. "I'm only telling you about it because I need your help."

Tom laughed. "Leave me out of it."

"Nee, Tom, you must listen to me. They'll get to know each other better at your birthday tomorrow night, and then I must arrange another meeting for them. I thought …"

"Why should I be involved, at all?"

"Just listen to me. I thought that you would be able to invite him to your place to fix something. I mean ask him if he might help you with something, so he thinks you're asking for his help. He won't say no. Then, while he's there, I'll just happen to visit with Mary Lou. While they're talking, you and I will disappear and leave them alone."

Tom pulled a face. "I do need someone to help me with the wall in my barn."

"Perfect!"

"Don't you want to know what's wrong with it?"

Emily laughed. "Not really."

"When did you say you're planning for this scheme of yours to take place?"

"I'm not certain yet. I'll let you know."

"I'll look forward to it."

"Does that mean you agree to it?" Emily asked.

"Only if it's just this once."

"It will be. *Denke,* Tom."

* * *

Emily had invited Tom's parents, some of her cousins, Mary Lou, and Luke to Tom's birthday dinner. She'd arranged for Tom to bring an extra table to the house to seat everyone. Now the two tables were arranged in a long row for the twenty guests. Emily and Deborah had cooked all of the food that Tom had brought over, and their cousins had also brought cooked food.

Luke's mother, who was conspiring in Emily's plan to match Luke and Mary Lou, had arranged for Luke to drive Mary Lou to and from the birthday dinner.

During the dinner, Tom was seated next to Luke and he asked him if he could help with the barn the following Thursday. Naturally, Luke had agreed. When the dinner was over, Tom had whispered to Emily that Luke had agreed to help him on Thursday.

Before the night was over, Mary Lou had agreed to spend Thursday with Emily and Deborah. The night had been a success in Emily's eyes.

* * *

Once most of the guests for the birthday dinner had left, Deborah walked upstairs exhausted. She collapsed onto her bed fully clothed and closed her eyes hoping to have a little nap and then she would have the energy to change for bed. Her baby was due anytime now. Molly had told her that a baby could be three weeks early or three weeks late, so her baby could arrive any day. She'd often had tightening sensations across her lower belly region, which Molly had said were 'practice contractions,' more commonly known as Braxton Hicks.

Even though she had a crib, diapers, and baby clothes ready, she didn't feel ready for the baby within herself. With Caleb dying, and adjusting to her new life without him, she hadn't enjoyed the pregnancy like she imagined she would've enjoyed it if Caleb had still been around.

Deborah smiled as she was sure she heard Emily talking to Tom downstairs. It sounded like they were having another one of their discussions about something.

Chapter 17

Fear thou not; for I am with thee:
be not dismayed; for I am thy God:
I will strengthen thee; yea, I will help thee;
yea, I will uphold thee with the right hand of my
righteousness.
Isaiah 41:10

When Thursday morning arrived, Emily intended to put the second phase of her plan into action. Deborah was going to be home all day, as the midwife was coming, and that would leave just Mary Lou and Emily to visit Tom. Of course, Emily would have to act shocked to see that Luke was at Tom's place on the very day they visited.

Emily had told Tom that, when they arrived, Tom and Luke should entertain the girls on the porch with iced tea, and after a few moments, Tom would tell Emily that he had to show her something in the barn.

"Are you nervous about the midwife's visit

today?" Emily asked Deborah.

"I'm trying my best to feel peaceful about it even though my stomach is churning."

"That's *gut. Dat* is going to spend all day making garden beds."

Deborah giggled. "Just another thing that Tom will have to finish off for him."

"Most likely," Emily agreed.

"I don't know what we'd do without Tom."

Emily nibbled on her bread and butter. She didn't know what she'd do without Tom either. What would she do if Tom suddenly became interested in a woman and no longer came around so often?

"What do you think, Emily?"

"What about?"

"I was talking about Tom. What a *gut* man he is."

"He is, he is for certain."

"What time is Mary Lou coming?"

Emily glanced at the clock on the shelf. "She should be here in an hour."

"What did you tell her you'd be doing with her

today?"

"I didn't really say. What should I do with her? We'll have two hours before we drive to Tom's."

"Maybe she will bring some sewing over and you can sew together."

"I didn't tell her to." Emily bit her lip. "It's been such a long time since I've had friends to the *haus.*"

"You should do it more often. You can't live your life around *Dat.* He won't be around forever."

Emily stared at her sister and knew she wouldn't be in the house forever either. She'd likely get married again. "I know that. I've just grown used to my own company and having Tom around here every day."

"Nothing stays the same, Emily. Tom will get married one day and won't be coming here so often. Not even to see *Dat.* If you like Tom, you should act now before it's too late."

Emily frowned and looked at her sister. "If I like Tom?"

"Jah. Do you?"

Emily bit her lip. "I don't know. I've been

157

thinking about him in a different way lately."

"Would you be upset if he married?"

Emily frowned. "That would be horrible."

"Then you must do something. You're used to having him around, and one day he might be gone. Don't take him for granted."

"Is that what I've been doing? I don't think we get along that well. He's always arguing with me."

Deborah laughed at her. "You know each other well. I think you do get along in your own way, just like Tom and his brother get along even though they're arguing. They're doing it in a friendly way."

"I don't think it's the same. They are joking with each other, and Tom gets frustrated with me."

"Well, just think about what I said, Emily."

"Denke, Deborah, I certainly will."

Chapter 18

Wealth gotten by vanity shall be diminished:
but he that gathereth by labour shall increase.
Proverbs 13:11

Later that day at Tom's house.

Once Emily was inside the barn, Tom closed them inside. Then Emily hurried to the window to look at Mary Lou and Luke on the porch, and Tom looked over her shoulder.

"It's all happening just as we'd planned."

"Just as *you'd* planned," Tom corrected her.

"They seem happy together. They're talking nicely. I wish we were close enough to hear what they're saying," Emily said.

"I think they're saying how obvious we made it when we left them alone."

"Very funny, Tom. They've got no idea that we set them up for this."

Tom and Emily continued to stare at them until Emily slapped Tom on his shoulder. "Did you see that? He must've said something funny because she laughed."

"Gut, can we go back now?"

"Nee, we must stay away and give them some more time to be alone."

"What am I supposed to be showing you in here? They might ask and we can't say different things."

Without taking her eyes off the couple, Emily said, "We'll say you were showing me the repairs that you and Luke did."

"They won't believe that."

"They will. Why would they doubt it?"

He grabbed her arm. "Well, we'll have to make it the truth. Come and have a look."

Emily giggled. "All right show me the work you've done." She followed Tom to the back of the barn into one of the stalls.

"See here?" He pointed to a hole in the wall. "We've patched one, but there's still one to go."

"How did it happen?"

"I had Hans Yoder's horse in here while he went away for a couple of days. He said the horse didn't get along with his other horses so he couldn't turn him lose in his paddock. Only thing was he didn't tell me that the horse likes to kick the walls of his stall. He didn't seem at all surprised when he came to collect him."

"Why didn't Hans help you fix it?"

"He was going to until you came up with the plan that I needed Luke here."

"Very clever."

He shook his head. "I can't believe that you've got me doing this kind of thing for you. When I'm very much against what you do."

"It'll all be worth it when they get married."

"You really think that will happen?" Tom rubbed his forehead.

"They like each other, don't you think?"

Tom nodded. "I do have to agree with you. There does appear to be a certain spark between them and I've never heard Luke so talkative."

"He's like that when he's away from his parents."

"How long must we stay in here?"

"Another ten minutes."

"Let's go out this way. They'll think we're still in the barn."

Tom opened a small doorway in the back of the barn, leading outside. They both had to crouch down to fit through. Once they were outside in the warm sunshine, Tom sat on a grassy patch in the field and Emily sat next to him.

"Have you ever thought that you like matching people because you yearn to get married yourself?" Tom asked.

While she was wondering how to answer him, he reached out and plucked a wildflower from the ground and handed it to her. She couldn't look at him although she could feel him staring at her. Her hand reached out, and she plucked the flower from his hands.

"It's pretty." She gazed at the yellow flower and in her nervousness started counting the petals in her mind. Once she reached twenty, he spoke again.

"You haven't answered me." He leaned slightly

closer.

Emily's throat constricted and she opened her mouth to gulp in air, which made her cough. He patted her on the back as she coughed again. "I'm all right." There was more silence and she knew she had to speak. "I don't think that's right."

"You don't want to get married someday?"

After another deep breath, she said, "I might someday." She looked down at the flower to see that she was twirling it nervously in her fingers.

"How about you, and I…"

Emily bounded to her feet. "I think we should go now. They must be wondering where we are by now."

He stood up. "It hasn't even been ten minutes."

Emily started walking towards the barn. "It doesn't need to be exactly ten, they've had enough time to get to know each other." She pushed her way through the small door in the barn, and when she was halfway to the main door, Tom caught up with her.

"Emily wait." He took hold of her arm and when

she stopped he let go.

She looked up into his face while she remembered everything her sister had said about Tom and losing him.

He pushed his hat back slightly. "This is hard for me to say."

Him being nervous immediately made her more at ease. "If you have something to say, then say it."

"I think what you're doing matching people together is silly, but I've seen it help bring people together who might not have otherwise come together."

"If you're going to speak to me, Tom, then speak plainly."

He smiled and the tension seemed to leave him. "You're a good kind person and that's the kind of person I'd like as my wife."

Emily raised her eyebrows.

He put his hand to his head. "You're making this hard for me."

A shaft of light falling through the barn interrupted them. They turned their heads to see that Luke and Mary Lou had come to find them.

"Here you are," Mary Lou said.

Chapter 19

There hath no temptation taken you
but such as is common to man:
but God is faithful,
who will not suffer you to be tempted
above that ye are able;
but will with the temptation also make a way to
escape, that ye may be able to bear it.
1 Corinthians 10:13

"*Jah,* I was showing Emily the work that Luke and I just did. We were just on our way back to the porch."

The four of them went back to sit on the porch. Emily stayed a few minutes longer before she and Mary Lou left to head back to her house.

"I think that Luke likes you," Emily said to Mary Lou.

"Do you? I do too, but I wasn't certain."

"I know he does. You both get along really well together."

"He's asked me on a buggy ride." Mary Lou giggled.

"Really? Of course, he likes you, then."

Mary Lou giggled again. "He's handsome don't you think?"

"*Jah,* he is."

"What was happening with you and Tom in the barn just now?" Mary Lou stared at Emily.

"Um, nothing."

Mary Lou wasn't fooled so easily. "There was so. I could see that we'd interrupted you. It looked like he was about to kiss you."

Now it was Emily's turn to giggle. "Mary Lou, don't say such things."

Mary Lou joined in her laughter. "He's quite a bit older than you, isn't he?"

"Only by a little bit." She recalled what Deborah had said about their age difference, and added, "Not enough to be a huge concern."

"So you like him?"

"Maybe I do, or maybe I don't."

"You don't want to tell me?"

She looked over at Mary Lou taking her eyes off the road for an instant. "It's not that I don't want to tell you, it's that I don't really know what I feel for him. A few weeks ago, he was nothing more than a close *familye* friend, but now I've started to look at him in a different way. I'm not entirely sure why, or what –if anything –has changed between us.

Mary Lou accepted what she said, and then nattered on about things, but Emily wasn't listening, all she could think about was Tom and what he'd been about to say to her.

When they got home, Mary Lou got in her buggy and left. Emily was relieved that she wouldn't have to entertain her any more that day. After Emily stood in the driveway and waved to Mary Lou, she unhitched the buggy, rubbed the horse down, and walked into the house.

Emily collapsed into the couch just as Deborah walked out of the kitchen.

"What's wrong with you?" Deborah asked.

"I'm exhausted."

Deborah sat next to her staring into her face.

"The matchmaking business must be tiring."

"It is, and not only that, something dreadful happened."

"What's wrong?"

"I think that Tom was going to ask me to marry him, or something."

Deborah's jaw dropped open. "Tell me exactly what he said."

"We were giving Mary Lou and Luke some time alone together and then we went to the barn. He handed me a flower and asked me what I thought about getting married. I can't remember exactly what he said, but I'm certain he was going to ask me to marry him, and then Mary Lou and Luke walked into the barn and he couldn't finish what he was going to say." Emily breathed out heavily.

"Why do you look so worried?"

"I don't know. It was kind of stressful." She stared at Deborah. "I was scared. What would I have said? I don't know how I feel. I've only just started to think about him in that way. I can't marry him before I know how I feel." Emily forced a laugh to hide her concern over her man troubles.

"You know what I mean?"

Deborah smiled. "It sounds like you're in love. It's exciting, and confusing sometimes too. It's especially like that before you talk about things together and he tells you how he really feels. If he'd told you how he felt today then you would be able to figure out how you feel about him."

"I'm scared."

"But excited too?"

Emily nodded.

"Don't worry so much. Things will happen how they're supposed to. Just enjoy watching how things unfold. Time goes by so quickly." She placed her hand over her stomach.

"Deborah! I'm sorry, I forgot to ask you how things went today with the midwife."

"They went well. The baby and I are fine."

* * *

That night, Deborah went to bed with thoughts of Caleb and their early romance on her mind.

She couldn't remember a time when Caleb was not in her life. They'd been raised in the same community and had gone to the same school. They had been together since they were sixteen and neither of them had been romantically interested in another. He'd even told her from a young age that he was going to marry her, and he'd been right. To be without him now didn't seem right. It was as though she was living someone else's life. She certainly felt as though she was somehow only half a person without Caleb in her life – with him she'd felt whole.

Deborah got out of bed and looked out the window at the moon. When she was younger, she would stare up at the moon and talk to her mother thinking she might be able to hear her.

It was then that Deborah made up her mind she should go to her mother's grave the very next day. She knew her mother was not in the grave, that she was with God, but the couple of times she'd visited the gravesite, she'd felt closer to her. She wondered if she should go by herself, or tell Emily where she was going. Emily might think it an odd thing to do, to talk to her mother as she sat by the grave. Deborah decided she needed to be alone at her mother's grave.

* * *

Deborah sat by her mother's headstone in the graveyard that was used by both Amish and Mennonite. Her mother's headstone was plain and rounded, and had her name, date of birth and the year she died.

"Hello, *Mamm,* if you can hear me. I'm having a *boppli*, as you probably already know, and Caleb's left me alone. I know I have to be strong and keep going, but I struggle daily with fearing more changes in my life. It seems nothing lasts forever, or stays the same, and that scares me. I don't know what I'd do if I lost *Dat,* but I know one day I will have to face that."

Sitting alone in the graveyard made Deborah

realize how brief the life of a human was. The Bible described it as a vapor, here one minute and gone the next. She had no power over when she was going to die or when her father was going to go, just as she'd had no choice in her mother going when she was such a young child.

Deborah breathed in deeply and was overcome with a sense of peace. The only thing she had control over was doing the best she could in this life, for her baby and for her family. She looked at the grave and ran two fingers over the grass that covered it.

"I'll see you again one day, *Mamm.* I've missed you and I've needed you, but for some reason I didn't get to have you around." She looked up to the sky and tried not to cry, but mostly when she thought about her mother that's exactly what she did. Deborah did not let herself look over at the other side of the graveyard where her husband was buried. Blocking out the pain of Caleb being gone was how she'd been coping lately.

Chapter 20

Come unto me, all ye that labour
and are heavy laden,
and I will give you rest.
Matthew 11:28

"Well, I have *gut* news," Tom said over dinner three nights later.

"We can always use some of that," Mr. Kauffman said.

Deborah and Emily leaned forward to hear what Tom had to say.

"It seems that Luke and Mary Lou are serious about each other. They've been seen together quite a bit." He looked directly at Emily.

"They've been seen out together so soon?" Emily asked, amazed.

Tom nodded. "You've done a *gut* job, Emily."

"*Denke,* Tom, I never thought I'd hear you say that. Did you hear what he said, Deborah?"

"*Jah,* I did. Why the big turnaround, Tom?

Didn't you recently accuse Emily of sticking her nose into other people's business?"

"Everyone's entitled to change their mind about things," Mr. Kauffman said.

"You two always stick together," Deborah said.

"As long as they both realize what I do is only to help people," Emily said as she glanced across the table at Tom.

* * *

Deborah knew her baby couldn't be too far away from arriving. The last couple of days the tightening episodes in her lower abdomen had become more frequent. Deborah wondered whether the Braxton Hicks were becoming real contractions, but she had no way to know.

Emily and Deborah were together at the farmers market getting some supplies when Deborah noticed the pains becoming stronger and more frequent.

"You told me you've been getting these pains for days, Deborah. Didn't the midwife say they weren't labor pains?"

"I don't know. These seem different and I have a feeling I need to get home."

"Okay, but I just want to call in and say hello to Tom –is that okay? It won't take long."

"All right, but we'll have to be quick."

As soon as they walked into the store, Deborah was gripped by a large contraction and had to lean against the doorway. She could hear Emily asking her what was wrong but she was in too much pain to answer.

Tom saw them and rushed over. When the pain stopped, Deborah looked up to see Nathan standing next to Tom.

"You're in labor," Nathan said.

"This is the first strong pain I've had."

"How long have you had this kind of pain?"

"I've been having small pains for weeks every now and again, but they've been getting stronger the last couple of days."

"And during these two days has Molly taken a look at you?"

"Nee. She told me this would happen the last few weeks, that I would have these practice pains. They've only been little twinges up until a few hours ago."

Nathan's lips pressed together. "Yes, but when you've had them so constantly they might be something else."

"I didn't know." Deborah was gripped by another contraction and Nathan took her arm so she could lean against him.

He looked across at Tom. "You'll need to call the midwife. Do you have the number?"

"I can find it," Tom said before he hurried away.

When the contraction passed, Deborah said, "That was a bad one."

Emily said to Nathan. "Is there anything I can do?"

"Not yet."

"Just stay close by me. Don't leave me," Deborah said.

Emily nodded.

Tom came back. "Molly's son answered the call and she's out on appointments. He's going to leave messages at all the places she's expected. We should hear from her soon."

"Can we use your backroom, Tom?"

"You can use my office."

When Deborah started walking toward Tom's office, she said, "I feel like I need to push."

"No, Not yet. Take short breaths during the contraction, and don't push," Nathan said."

Tears streamed down Deborah's face, she didn't want to have the baby in a furniture store, or without the midwife she knew and trusted. Things were not working out how she had envisioned they would.

When the urge to push had passed, Deborah walked into Tom's office with Emily and Nathan. Tom cleared everything off his office desk and then walked out. Nathan spotted a pump bottle of antibacterial solution, cleaned his hands, and then he called Tom back and whispered to him, "Call 911."

Deborah overheard. "Is something wrong with the baby, just tell me?"

"Nothing is wrong; it's just I'll feel better if I have some help delivering your baby."

Deborah gasped. "You're going to do it?"

"If I have to, then, yes."

"Have you done it before? Isn't your specialty at the other end of the body?" Emily asked.

"I had to learn how to deliver babies in my general training. I've seen babies being born before."

"Have you delivered one yourself before?" Emily asked.

"I've delivered plenty of calves over the years when they got stuck."

"I'm not a cow," Deborah yelled as she was gripped by another urge to push.

Chapter 21

And he said unto me,
My grace is sufficient for thee:
for my strength is made perfect in weakness.
Most gladly therefore will I rather glory in my
infirmities,
that the power of Christ may rest upon me.
2 Corinthians 12:9-10

"Don't push! Not yet," Nathan said firmly.

"You tell this baby not yet," Deborah managed to say.

"They're not far away," Tom said from the other side of the door.

"Hear that, Deborah? Help's coming," Emily said.

"I've done the training, Deborah. I need to see if you're fully dilated before you can push."

"My baby's coming now?"

Nathan smiled at her, and nodded. "It seems so, if you're feeling the urge to push."

Deborah agreed to have him examine her and he told her she could push now.

As soon as she sat up, she was gripped by another strong contraction and she couldn't do anything else but push.

When the contraction was finished, he said, "I think you're only another few pushes away. I can see about two inches of your baby's head."

Deborah looked over at Emily who had tears pouring out of her eyes.

"Everything will be okay, Deborah. I'm sorry I didn't leave for home earlier like you wanted to."

"By the looks of it, you might have had the baby on the roadside if you had. Emily, have Tom send someone to buy towels from somewhere, and cotton sheets, and tell them to hurry."

"Don't go," Deborah called out.

"I'll just tell Tom, and I'll be right back," Emily said before she slipped through the door. Emily was back in the room within thirty seconds. "See, I'm back again."

"Come stand by me and hold my hand."

Emily stood next to her and grabbed her hand. Deborah clutched her tightly as soon as she was gripped by another urge to push.

"I need to push." After bearing down, which seemed to last forever, her baby slithered into Nathan's hands.

She watched Nathan's face as he beamed with delight. "You have a boy."

"Is he okay?" Deborah asked, trying to see the baby.

"He seems healthy. He's just taken a breath all on his own. Emily, see how they're doing with those towels and things."

Emily slipped out the door. With the umbilical cord still attached, Nathan passed the baby to Deborah.

Deborah held the slippery baby in her arms. "He's perfect. He's looking at me. And he's got all his fingers and toes." She clutched the baby to her chest and knew she'd never feel alone again.

"He's a beautiful boy," Nathan said.

"He's not crying."

"As long as he's breathing there's no need to cause him to cry. He'll cry when he's ready."

The paramedics came through the door and immediately Nathan gave them an update on Deborah and the baby's condition.

While one took Deborah's blood pressure, the other placed a blanket over the baby.

Nathan rubbed his forehead and collapsed on the couch on the other side of the office. The paramedics asked Deborah if she wanted to cut the cord. She was too overwhelmed with everything to do it.

When the paramedics left some twenty minutes later, Emily came back into the office.

"I'm sorry I had to leave; there wasn't enough room for everyone in here."

"You were here when I needed you, that's what's important," Deborah said.

Emily peered down at the baby. "A little boy. He's so tiny."

"He's perfect."

"You didn't wait for me," the midwife said as she walked in.

Deborah smiled at her. "This one didn't wait. I was happy to wait. Nathan delivered the baby."

She hurried over to look at the baby and as she did so she glanced across at Nathan, "Hello, Nathan, I haven't seen you in years. It was good that you could get here so quickly."

"I happened to be here when she came to the store heavily in labor. The paramedics checked her and the baby over, and they're both doing fine. I expect you'll visit Deborah every day for the next couple of weeks?" Nathan asked.

"Naturally," she said. Molly looked at the baby. "He's beautiful and he looks a good size too."

Nathan jumped to his feet, walked over and kissed Deborah's forehead. "Congratulations, Deborah."

"Thank you, Nathan. I don't know what I would've done if you weren't here."

He chuckled. "You were the one who did all the work. I better go now or I'll be late for work. I'll come to visit and check on this little guy in the next day or two if that's alright by you?"

"You're welcome always," Deborah said.

"Is it safe to come in now?"

Deborah looked up to see Tom in the doorway. *"Jah,* new *onkles* are allowed in now." Tom walked into the room as Nathan walked out.

Tom had a look at the baby and as soon as he did so the baby screwed up his face and cried. Tom laughed. "I usually have that effect on women - babies not so much."

"If everyone will leave Deborah and me alone now, that would be good," Molly said. Once everyone was gone, the midwife checked Deborah and the baby over. She helped Deborah settle her son for his first feeding, to quiet his cries.

Two hours later, Deborah's father was in the store, having heard the news.

By this time Tom's office was cleaned up, Deborah and Emily were on the couch and Emily was holding the baby.

He walked over to them and he kissed Deborah on the cheek. "This was a *gut* surprise. My first *grosskinner.*"

Emily stood up with the baby in her arms. "You want to hold him, *Dat?*"

"I would very much like to hold him."

When her father sat on the other end of the couch, Emily handed the baby to him. The baby was snug in a cotton wrap that the midwife had brought with her.

Tears came to their father's eyes. "Your *mudder* would have loved to be here right now."

Deborah put her head on her father's shoulder. The girls had never seen him cry before. "She'll meet him one day, *Dat,*" Deborah said.

He nodded. "I know." After a while, he looked at Deborah. "Let me know when you're ready to go home. You look exhausted."

"I'm ready now, *Dat.*"

"I'll follow you, Deborah, and stay for the day to make sure you're okay. You can have a sleep and I'll watch the *boppli,*" Molly said.

"That sounds perfect, Molly."

* * *

Deborah went home with their father, ahead of Emily.

"I suspect you never thought *that* would happen today, Tom," Emily said.

"That was the last thing I expected to happen today." Emily didn't want to leave Tom. "Will I see you tonight?" "I think I'll leave your *familye* in peace for the next few nights." Emily knew the disappointment was evident on her face.

"Perhaps instead of me making a nuisance of myself at your *haus,* you might come out to dinner with me tomorrow night?" Emily smiled. "I'd like that." She knew this wasn't the time for jokes or sarcasm.

"I'll come by and get you at six?"

Emily nodded. "Perfect."

"How are you getting home?" Tom asked.

"I've got my buggy just around the corner.

That's how we came here, Deborah and I. I'll see you tonight then, I mean tomorrow."

Tom flashed her a smile and she walked away and headed to her buggy.

* * *

Deborah managed to have some sleep that afternoon while her baby slept for a few hours. After the midwife left, he'd cried on and off until eight o'clock, and then he went to sleep again. It was now nine and Deborah's body was tired, but she felt a sense of peace at the same time.

It would've been nice if her mother and Caleb could've seen the baby, but that's not what God had planned and she did her best to accept that.

The baby woke again at ten, and after he was fed and had his diaper changed, he fell back to sleep. The pattern was repeated twice during the night.

When the baby cried again, Deborah was pleased to see daylight. She'd made it through the first night. She got out of bed and walked over to the crib. "Hello, my *bu,* welcome to your second day in the world." She picked him up and he looked right into her eyes. "You have got to be the most beautiful *boppli* that there ever was." She kissed him on his bald head.

Hanging over her head was the appointment she'd made with Caleb's specialist as soon as she and Caleb had told him that she was pregnant. The doctor was keen to have the baby tested just in case the baby might be afflicted with what Caleb had. Even if the baby would be given the all-clear, she knew she'd have to have him back to be checked regularly. Both of Caleb's parents had died young, but Caleb's sister was still fine.

Chapter 22

Be of good courage,
and he shall strengthen your heart,
all ye that hope in the Lord.
Psalms 31:24

Emily had been a bundle of nerves since Tom had asked her out. This was to be the first time she'd be out alone with a man on a date. Now there was no secret; she knew that he liked her, and she guessed he knew by her acceptance of the dinner invitation that those feelings were returned.

What had started out as a relationship between friends was developing into something more. Previously she wouldn't have cared what he thought of her or her opinions, but now, what he thought or said mattered.

She made dinner for Deborah and her father before she left. She walked into the living room where her father sat. "I'm going soon, *Dat.*" She sat down next to him.

"I've got soup on the stove, there's warm bread in the oven, and some small apple tarts for dessert."

"You didn't need to do that. I could've found something to get for Deborah and me to eat."

"It was no trouble."

"Where are you and Tom going?"

"I don't know; we're going out for dinner somewhere."

Her father nodded and she knew that he was pleased that she and Tom were growing closer. He'd be pleased if she married Tom, since Tom was his closest friend. Emily wondered if her father ever brought to mind the days when he and her mother were courting. He'd never told her or her sister any stories of those days and she was reluctant to ask in case the memories were too painful for him.

"That might be him now," he said.

"Could be. I'll just go up and see if Deborah wants me to do something before I leave." Emily raced up the stairs and ran into Deborah's room. "Tom's nearly here. Do you want me to do anything before I leave? I've got dinner on the stove and

I've told *Dat* what to do with it."

"*Nee* you just go and have a good time and don't hurry home. We're fine here."

"Okay." Emily kissed the baby in Deborah's arms, and then kissed her sister on the cheek. "I'll tell you all about it when I get home."

Deborah was quick to say, "Only if I'm awake, otherwise let me sleep. He woke three or four times last night."

"I won't wake you." Emily rushed downstairs, straightened her prayer *kapp,* pinched her cheeks to give her pale face some color, and then spread a little oil on her lips so they would look shiny. She slung her shawl over her shoulders and walked to the door. She opened it just as Tom was about to knock.

He looked down at her and smiled. "Are you ready?"

"I'm all ready to go."

Tom stuck his head in the door to wave to her father. Emily hoped her father wouldn't strike up a conversation because she was anxious to be alone with Tom. Thankfully he didn't.

They climbed into the buggy and Tom turned it around and headed back down the driveway.

"How's the new *boppli?*" he asked.

"Very good. Molly came today and said everything is going fine. It was good that your *bruder* was visiting you at the store just at the right time."

"*Jah, Gott* plans everything perfectly."

"I suppose that's right; it wasn't a coincidence or good fortune. It was all in His plan."

A little while later, Tom said, "I hope you like Mexican food?"

Emily scrunched up her nose. "I don't know. I've never had it before."

"I think you'll like it. If not, we'll go somewhere different."

"I'm sure I'll like it." She wished she could relax and be herself but she was too nervous.

He looked at her. "Are you okay?"

"*Jah.* I think I'm just a little tired. I've been helping with the baby a lot."

"I guess that would be tiring."

"He woke a lot during the night, but I was fast asleep. Deborah's really tired."

"It's a good thing she's got you to help her, with Caleb gone. Speaking of Caleb, Nathan mentioned to me that your sister should take the baby to the hospital to make sure he doesn't have the same illness as his father."

"I heard her talking to Molly about that. I will remind her."

"Hopefully he'll be okay."

"I hope so."

Tom parked the buggy close to the Mexican restaurant. It felt strange to Emily to be out with Tom after all the years of having dinner with him at her house.

He held the door of the restaurant open for her while she walked through first. The waiter seated them at a corner table where a white candle flickered in the center. Emily wondered whether he'd called ahead and asked for a table with privacy.

He looked down at the menu. "I guess you don't

know what anything's like so I'll order us a few dishes, and then you can try some of each."

"Sounds good." She folded up her menu and placed it on the table in front of her. When the waiter came back to take the order, Emily tried to keep her nerves in check. She was normally a bold confident person but now she was out of her depth. When the waiter left with their order, she searched her mind for something to talk to Tom about. "I hope you didn't lose too many customers yesterday."

He laughed. "Wednesdays are usually quiet anyway, so it didn't matter. Does he have a name yet?"

"Nee. Deborah is thinking hard about it and has a few options but hasn't let anyone know what they are."

"Tom's a good name," he said straight-faced.

Emily laughed. "You would think so."

"It's a good upstanding name. Thomas." He laughed, and then got more serious. "I'm glad we can be alone. We're normally surrounded by so many people at your *haus."*

Not knowing how to respond, she thought it best to talk about other people. "So how long do you think it will take Marylou and Luke to get married?"

"I think they'll probably get married soon. At their age they don't have a lot of time to waste."

Emily laughed. "Aren't you older than Luke?"

"Of course, but age doesn't matter to me. If it did, I wouldn't be sitting across from you now."

"Do you think we have a large age difference?"

"Nee it's not so great. When two people get along it shouldn't matter how old they are."

"That's true."

A waiter brought a jug of iced water to the table with two glasses. "Are you having wine this evening?" the waiter asked.

Tom looked at Emily. "Wine?"

Emily shook her head. "Not for me." She knew wine was the last thing she needed right now.

Tom looked up at the waiter. "We're fine with water, thank you."

When the waiter was gone, Tom said, "My guess is that Luke will be married in six months time."

"I think it'll be one month."

"Nee, it'll be six. You can't know everything, Emily."

"I'm good about these kinds of things. You have to trust me; I haven't been wrong before."

"What about the time you thought Luke and Deborah would be *gut* together."

Emily laughed. "That was a mistake."

"Denke. I'm glad you admit to making them."

"Tell me, I've always wanted to know something. Why do you and *Dat* like whittling so much?"

"It's not to make things as much as it is calming for our minds. I guess it takes your *vadder* and me back to our childhoods. We both enjoyed whittling as young boys; many men like to whittle. All you need is a knife and some soft wood. We started out using pine or balsa off-cuts, but now we like using odd-looking branches or twigs."

Emily shook her head. "I don't think I'll ever understand the attraction of it."

After a while, Emily found herself relaxing and she could finally be herself. They stayed at the restaurant until they were nearly the last ones to leave.

"So you found out tonight that you do like Mexican food?" Tom asked.

"*Jah,* I do; very much. The tortillas with the fish inside were my favorite."

"I might bring you here again if you behave yourself." He smiled at Emily. "We should go. I think they'll most likely kick us out if we don't leave now."

It was then that Emily got nervous again and she stayed nervous right until Tom's buggy pulled up at her house. She didn't know if he might try to kiss her when they said goodnight. And if so, what would she do?

When he pulled the buggy up at the *haus,* she jumped out immediately, and then turned to face him. "Do you want to come in for a while, Tom?"

Tom had made no attempt to get out of the buggy. "*Nee,* it's late. I'll see you soon."

"Okay, bye, Tom. *Denke* for a lovely night." She hurried to the house.

Chapter 23

But they that wait upon the Lord shall renew their
strength; they shall mount up with wings as eagles;
they shall run, and not be weary;
and they shall walk, and not faint.
Isaiah 40:31

A month later, they were all sitting at the wedding of Luke and Mary Lou. During the ceremony, Emily turned around from her seat and smirked at Tom. She'd been right; they'd only taken one month to get married.

Emily turned her attention back to the front of the room where Luke and Mary Lou were seated.

It hadn't been so long ago that they were at the wedding of Harriet and Michael. Back then she'd had no thought that Tom and she might have gotten along so well.

She turned around the other way to look at her sister a few rows behind her, holding baby Caleb Nathan King in her arms. Deborah smiled back at her. Emily had thought that Deborah might name the baby Caleb, but it was a surprise to everyone that his middle name was Nathan, after Tom's brother.

Emily turned back to the front when the bishop pronounced Luke and Mary Lou married. Before she knew it, everyone was moving out of Mary Lou's parents' home where the wedding was being held. She rose to her feet, and just as she did so, Tom stood right by her.

"I can see you're looking pretty pleased with yourself."

"Jah. I was right about a lot of things."

"Might I remind you that you first thought that Deborah and Luke would've made a good pair?"

"Okay, I know that would've been wrong. No need to keep reminding me."

"Are you saying that you were wrong?" he pulled on his ear and bent over.

Emily laughed at him. *"Nee,* not totally. I was just thinking out aloud about the two of them. I hadn't fully decided."

Emily saw Mrs. Hostetler looking around for people to help with the food. She grabbed Tom's arm. "Quick let's get out of here. I can't let Mrs. Hostetler see me or she'll have me washing dishes and I'll have no fun at all."

As they wandered over to the refreshments table, Tom said, "Marry me, Emily."

She stopped and looked up into his face. He was serious. They'd been on a date every week over the last four weeks, and she'd started hoping like crazy for him to ask her this very thing. "Are you asking me, or are you ordering me? Because that didn't sound like a question."

"Emily Kauffman, you're an impossible woman, but because I like to figure out difficult puzzles and how things work, I think you might be entertaining to have as a *fraa.*" He laughed. "Emily Kauffman, will you please marry me and make me a very happy man?"

Although many people were around, it felt to Emily as though they were alone. She nodded. "I will marry you, Tom, I will."

He smiled wider, and then said, "Come with me." He walked quickly and Emily had to nearly run to catch up to him.

"Where are you taking me?"

He didn't answer until they were around the corner of the barn. He placed his arms around her and she melted against his body. "I've waited a long time to have my arms around you."

With her eyes shut tightly and her head feeling his fast-beating heart, she could barely speak. She stepped back quickly. "Someone might see us."

"I don't care. Let's get married in a month." He picked up her hand and held it in both of his. "If Luke and Mary Lou could talk the Bishop into marrying them so quickly, I think he'll do the same for us."

"You want to get married so soon?"

"I do."

Before she stepped into his arms once more, she nodded in agreement.

Chapter 24

While the earth remaineth, seedtime and harvest, and
cold and heat, and summer and winter, and day and
night shall not cease.
Genesis 8:20

As Deborah walked away from the celebration and toward the buggy, she looked around for Emily and couldn't see her anywhere. The baby needed feeding and changing and she'd have to do all that in the buggy. Just as she reached the buggy, she glanced around and saw Emily and Tom in an embrace behind the barn.

Gladness filled Deborah's heart and she smiled: they made such a lovely couple. Emily had confessed she wanted more than anything to marry Tom, and Deborah hoped he'd ask her soon.

As she sat in the buggy feeding the baby, she wondered what life would be like if Emily moved out of the house to live with Tom. She and the baby would be left alone with her father. The house would be a lot quieter without Emily around, but at least she wouldn't be moving too far and maybe both she and Tom would come over for dinner all the time.

A minute later, Deborah looked up to see Emily hurrying toward her.

She stuck her head into the buggy, and said breathlessly, "Tom and I are getting married."

"Emily, that's such good news."

"I know, I'm so happy I think that I'll burst. And Tom wants to get married as soon as we can. In just one month; can you believe it? Just one month."

"I'm so happy for you."

"I never thought I'd be married. I thought maybe one day I suppose, but I never knew it would be to Tom, and I never knew it would be this fast "

"I can tell you and Tom have something special together."

Emily looked down at Caleb. "This time next year I might have my own *boppli.*"

"That would be *gut* and then they could grow up together. Have you told anyone else you and Tom are getting married?"

"*Nee* he just asked me now. He's coming to dinner tonight to tell *Dat.*"

"*Dat* won't be too surprised and he won't object. He doesn't say much, but he knows everything that's going on. He'll be delighted. I don't think you could've found anyone better to marry, in his eyes."

* * *

It was five weeks later when Deborah was sitting with Caleb on her lap watching her younger sister and Tom get married.

The last wedding that had taken place in her father's house was her wedding to Caleb. She closed her eyes and remembered her wedding and recalled looking into Caleb's eyes and knowing that they'd be happy for the rest of their lives.

Pulling her mind back to the present, Deborah concentrated on her sister's wedding to Tom. This was going to be one of the most important days in her sister's life and she was pleased to be there for it.

She looked over at Tom's brother, Nathan. He had visited the house twice since Caleb was born. He'd become a friend, and Deborah felt a bond with him in a strange way since he'd been there to help with the birth of her baby. Knowing that she found a space in her heart that she never knew existed for Caleb, she wondered if she might find another space, and love once more in her lifetime.

Her baby started to cry, so she jiggled him up and down on her lap, which made him stop. She didn't want to take him outside and miss the wedding. Glancing again at Nathan, she finally admitted to herself that it would feel nice to have a man's arms around her once more. She'd always felt so safe and protected when she'd been in Caleb's strong arms.

Smiling, she looked down at her baby lying comfortably in her lap. It was a blessing to watch him grow. He now had some dark hair coming through, and his cheeks were getting chubbier every day. Nothing mattered to her except that he was healthy. It had only been a week since her baby was tested at the hospital, and he had no signs of the illness that had taken his father away. There were no guarantees in life – she'd come to learn that from growing up without a mother and having her husband taken from her. She'd take what daily blessings came her way.

Deborah sniffed back tears, and then wiped one that fell down her cheek. She'd been blessed with a son, and she thanked God for what she'd been given, and then she also thanked God for the family that remained with her. As for her mother and Caleb, they were now safe in God's house; He had wanted them home.

* * *

When the ceremony had nearly come to an end, Mrs. Hostetler and a few of the ladies raced into the kitchen to prepare all the food to feed the hundreds of guests.

Finally, the bishop announced Tom and Emily as a married couple. Emily glanced at her father and saw the joy on his face. Before she turned back to the front to look at her new husband, Nathan caught her attention. What better man would there be for her sister than Nathan, the man who had helped bring her child into the world? It was also good that Nathan was Tom's brother. Even though Nathan wasn't in the community right now that didn't mean that he'd be out forever.

Tom and Emily walked outside to the wedding table where they would sit with their attendants to eat the meal afterward.

Mrs. Hostetler hurried over to Emily, wagging her finger at her. "You missed out on helping us this time, Emily, but I'll find you at the next wedding. I can't ask you to help us do the washing up at this wedding because it's your own."

Emily laughed. "I'll wash up at the next one, Mrs. Hostetler. As long as it's not my *schweschder's.*"

Mrs. Hostetler's eyes opened wide. "Deborah's getting married?"

"Not that I know of. I think we're fairly safe."

Mrs. Hostetler looked a little confused, then hurried back into the house.

"Looks like she finally caught up with you," Tom whispered.

"I told you she doesn't like me."

Tom laughed.

"What do you think about your *bruder* and my *schweschder?*" Emily whispered.

"A bad idea; a very bad idea."

"What's wrong with that? I think they'd make a lovely couple."

"He's not in the community and she'd be unequally yoked with an unbeliever."

"He might come back."

"*Nee*, never. He made his decision a long time ago, and that's his choice. Neither you or I can change his mind for him."

Emily pouted. "I just want her to be happy."

"She's happy; look at her."

Emily saw her sister talking to other women with babies the same age as Caleb. She certainly did look happy as she talked with them.

"All right, I won't do anything about her and your *bruder,* but that doesn't mean that I'll stop looking for someone who's absolutely perfect for her."

"Nee, don't. If *Gott* wants it to happen it will. Maybe it's time to put your attention elsewhere. Like focus it on me."

Emily frowned at him.

He shook his head at her. "I can see I'll have to keep you very busy. We'll have to have lots of *kinner* so you'll stop this matchmaking nonsense if for no other reason than you'll have no time for it."

"I like the sound of that."

"Focusing on me?"

"Nee, of course not. Having lots of *kinner."*

"That's one thing we agree on and that's a *gut* start to our married life." He smiled and stared into her eyes. "I wonder if it would be too shocking if we kissed right now."

"Nee, we couldn't!"

He laughed. "All right, but we're leaving here as soon as it's polite to do so and then I'm going to kiss you as soon as we're in the buggy."

"And that's another thing we agree on." Emily looked into her husband's handsome face and didn't know if her life could get any better. Once she'd taken Tom for granted, but she'd never do it again. Every day she would tell herself to thank God for every blessing that came her way.

Chapter 25

*Being confident of this very thing, that he which hath
begun a good work in you will perform it until the day
of Jesus Christ:*
Philippians 1:6

Deborah held her baby in one arm and spread the blanket she'd brought with her with her other hand. When she'd spread the last corner of the blanket out with her foot, she sat in the middle with her son in her arms. She looked over at her father driving away in the buggy and wondered what he thought of her coming to the graveyard like this; she was glad he hadn't given his opinion. He'd agreed to come back in one hour to collect them.

Now she felt ready to talk to Caleb and face the fact that he was gone and she and baby Caleb were alone. All the feelings she'd suppressed over the past months came flooding back and she was unable to do anything but cry. Six-month-old

Caleb knew there was something different about his mother today and he stared up at her, concerned and curious.

Once Deborah looked at her baby she said, "It's all right my *boppli;* we're here with your *vadder.* " It was then she felt she was able to say a few words to Caleb just as she had spoken to her mother at her gravesite from time to time. "Caleb, this is your son. He looks like you and what better name could I have called him but your name?"

Deborah gave a laugh as she imagined Caleb and their baby interacting. She looked down at her baby boy. "We're close to your *Dat.* He loves you very much and always will." He stared into her face as though trying to comprehend what she was saying. "You'll understand me one day, and I'll tell you all about your *vadder.* " With her sleeve she wiped more tears that fell from her eyes.

"What do you think of our *boppli,* Caleb? He's truly a miracle. *Gott* has left me with part of you as a comfort to me. I don't want to go on without you but the choice has not been mine. Now I have to be a *gut mudder* to our son."

She could feel Caleb with her. Closing her eyes she imagined his arms encircling her and their baby; peace filled her heart. At that moment, as though a light had been switched on inside her, she knew that their love would never fade because it was eternal. She breathed out with relief and as she did so she felt all the heaviness in her heart float upward.

It had taken a while, but now she felt she could face the world without him knowing that their love would never die.

* * *

Almost a year to the day after Emily and Tom had married, Emily was sitting with Caleb on her lap and waiting for Deborah to be married. Caleb had been running around all morning and had exhausted himself, and Emily was pleased that it now looked as though he would sit quietly through his mother's wedding.

Tom leaned over toward her. "Looks like she's changed her mind."

"Hush, Tom. You're just cross because I proved you wrong again."

Tom chuckled. "I hoped when you found we were having a *boppli* that you'd give up your matchmaking."

"I can't. I told you before, it's what I'm *gut* at."

"Well, where's Deborah?"

"Maybe I should go up and see if she's okay."

"And risk livening Caleb up again? That's not a *gut* idea. She'll be down soon."

Emily nodded and looked over to the front where the bishop and one of the deacons were sitting. The wedding was about to take place in her father's house; the same place where she had been married, and also where Deborah's first wedding had taken place.

Deborah had told her many times that she never intended to marry again, but Emily had seen a definite spark between Deborah and Nathan right from the very beginning. The fact that Emily's new brother-in-law, and the fact that she and Tom frequently ate dinner with her sister and their father, had made it easy for Emily to arrange many meetings between the pair.

* * *

Deborah sat on her bed by herself in her bedroom. She knew she should go downstairs because everyone was most likely waiting for her. A couple of moments to herself was what she needed. Never in a million years did she even imagine that she would marry again, but Nathan just fitted into her life perfectly. When she agreed to marry him, he bought a house close to Tom's, and had spoken to the bishop. The bishop had agreed for Nathan to come back to the community and be baptized.

Because of Nathan's profession, he'd been given permission to use a computer and a phone inside his house so the hospital could have a line of communication with him. Nathan was often on call.

Everything had worked out perfectly for the couple. Emily had kept telling Deborah that things would work out. Deborah hadn't imagined that Nathan would ever want to come back to the community, let alone that the bishop would allow him so many privileges to continue his work.

Deborah rose to her feet and took in a big breath before she walked to the window. Looking out over the fields, she was pleased that all guilt had left her. She'd struggled with finding herself falling in love with Nathan, thinking she was betraying her love for Caleb. After her visit to Caleb's grave, she'd realized that her late-husband would've wanted her to continue her life –to go on and be happy. Nathan made her happy, and Nathan had a bond with her son.

Rather than suffering with feelings of guilt, Deborah was now suffering with nerves that made her stomach churn. She wondered how things would work. Would Nathan feel too constricted by the Amish life, even though he'd been given privileges? He'd been living the Amish life for three months in the house he'd bought for them and so far everything seemed fine. He'd go to work in a taxi and put on his white coat, do his work, and come home by taxi. His life at work remained unchanged. The bishop had warned Nathan that he shouldn't be coming back for Deborah, and Nathan had insisted he was returning to the Amish for his own salvation. He said that the gift of helping at Caleb's birth had opened his heart so he could hear God calling him back to his Amish roots.

It was then that Deborah realized she was nervous because of change. She was a creature of habit and didn't do well with change – she feared it. Whenever she was afraid, she prayed. Closing her eyes, she again placed her life in God's hands and thanked Him for all He'd done for her. She had a wonderful baby boy, a good family, and now God had blessed her with a second love. It was a miracle, and not only that, Nathan was now a believer and that probably wouldn't have happened if she and her baby hadn't come into his life. Opening her eyes again, she could see that God had planned all of this from the beginning.

Placing her hand over her heart, she told herself to calm down. She'd have to put her nerves aside and put one foot in front of the other, and walk downstairs toward the man she loved and toward her future. She knew that Nathan and she were right for each other.

* * *

Tom leaned over, "Here she comes."

Emily turned around to see Deborah join Nathan at the bottom of the stairs. It melted Emily's heart when she saw the loving way they looked into each other's eyes. Together they walked to the front where the bishop waited for them.

"Mamm, Mamm," Caleb called out when he saw his mother.

"Shh," Emily whispered, "*Mamm* is getting

married. You have to be a *gut bu* and keep quiet." When her words didn't prevent Caleb from calling out, Emily produced a cookie and handed it to Caleb. Even though Deborah said he shouldn't eat too many, Emily could see it was the only way he was going to keep quiet throughout the ceremony.

Tears streamed down Emily's face when Deborah and Nathan were finally married. And what's more, Tom had told her twelve months ago that it would never happen.

Deborah turned around and put her arms out to Caleb, so Emily let him run to her. Once she'd picked him up, Deborah, Nathan and Caleb headed out to where the tables for the reception were set up.

"Let's go," Tom said to Emily. While on their way outside, Tom stared at her. "I've never seen you cry."

She sniffed. "I do sometimes."

Tom laughed. "I do have to say that you were right about Nathan and Deborah even though I was convinced the whole thing would never happen.

Now that you've had another success, will you give up and concentrate on having our *boppli?* The birth's not that far away. You could paint the nursery or make curtains."

"I might do that." Emily looked around and saw her father talking to Molly, the midwife. Molly had never married and she was so nice; she'd be perfect for their father. And, Emily could invite her father over on the days when Molly was due to make house visits to check on her pregnancy.

Tom followed her gaze. "Who are you looking at now?"

"I'm just looking at *Dat.* Nothing for you to be concerned with."

Tom smiled, and shook his head at her once more.

For I know the thoughts that I think toward you,
saith the LORD, thoughts of peace,
and not of evil, to give you an expected end.
Jeremiah 29:11

* * * * * * * * * *

For updates on

Samantha Price's NEW RELEASES,

and GIVEAWAYS subscribe to the email

newsletter at :

http://www.samanthapriceauthor.com

Also in this series

Book 1

Amish Widow's Hope

Newly widowed Amish woman, Anita Graber, has returned to live with her brother and his family in Lancaster County. As an expectant widow, she is quite surprised when everyone from the bishop's wife to her brother decides that her baby needs a father. Anita endures many embarrassing moments as she's forced into one awkward situation after another. Even though another man is the last thing on her mind, she finds a friend in her sister-in-law's brother, Simon. Anita wonders why everyone has rejected Simon as a suitable match for her.

Will Anita finally convince everyone that she

and her baby are happy on their own?

Could the man that no one sees her with, be the very man who eventually captures her heart?

Book 2

The Pregnant Amish Widow

After her husband's death, Grace Stevens returns to her family and her Amish community. She'd suffered through an abusive marriage and wanted nothing more than to be baptized into the Amish faith and begin a new life.

Grace finds it impossible to put the past behind her when Marlene, the woman who caused her to leave the community, was now living in Grace's family home and married to Grace's brother.

More friction occurs between the women when Grace discovers that she's five months pregnant. As Marlene is childless after four years of marriage, she spirals further into depression.

When Grace learns that the man she nearly married is still single, she wonders if they might rekindle what they once had, but her hopes fade when she learns she's not the only woman interested in him.

Can Grace come to terms with having her late husband's baby, forgive Marlene enough to comfort her, and secure the love of the man she once loved so dearly?

Samantha loves to hear from her readers.

Connect with Samantha Price at:

samanthaprice333@gmail.com

http://twitter.com/AmishRomance

http://www.facebook.com/SamanthaPriceAuthor

56088505R00127

Made in the USA
Charleston, SC
14 May 2016